Redeeming
THE
COWBOY
BLACKWATER RANCH BOOK SIX

MANDI BLAKE

Redeeming the Cowboy
Blackwater Ranch Book Six
By Mandi Blake

Copyright © 2021 Mandi Blake
All Rights Reserved

Published in the United States of America
Cover Image Photographer: Macie May's Photography
Cover Model: Daryl Abbott
Cover Designer: Amanda Walker PA & Design
Services
Editor: Editing Done Write
Ebook ISBN: 978-1-953372-09-3
Paperback ISBN: 978-1-953372-13-0

Acknowledgments

I have loved writing this series, but I couldn't have done it alone. I'm blessed to have a wonderful team of friends who help me craft each book.

Thanks to Stephanie Martin, Hannah Jo Abbott, Elizabeth Maddrey, Kendra Haneline, and Jess Mastorakos for guiding me through the confusing author world. It's great to have friends who aren't afraid to tell me the truth, even if it's not what I want to hear. That kind of trust is rare, and I wouldn't trade our friendship for anything.

My beta readers, Pam Humphrey, Tanya Smith, and Jenna Eleam know how to make all of the books I write better, and I'm grateful for their advice and counsel. I appreciate my ARC readers who send me any typos that snuck through the editing process and share their opinions and reviews of the books.

My editor, Brandi Aquino of Editing Done Write, and my cover designer, Amanda Walker, know how to make a finished book look wonderful. They're so good at what they do, and I'm thankful for our friendship and being able to work with them on this journey.

When I needed a cover model for this book, the talented Macie Shubert was there to make it happen. She introduced me to Daryl Abbott, who is the perfect cowboy for this book cover, and his lovely wife, Jenna Abbott.

As always, Dana Burttram keeps her patience with me as I pepper her with questions about law enforcement protocols. Kim Barker is my go-to for medical questions, and she's also one of the reasons I love reading so much. God knew what he was doing when he gave me these two aunts.

Last, but not least, thank you reader for taking a chance on my books. Writing these stories is a dream come true, and it means so much to me that you support me. I always love hearing your thoughts about the books, so please reach out if you have something to say!

Contents

Chapter One

FELICITY

Felicity stood just outside the doorway of Dawn's bedroom but couldn't step over the threshold. It had been a week since Dawn died, but the pain in Felicity's chest had been so unrelenting that she couldn't remember a time when the ache hadn't existed, ruling her life and sucking the joy out of every minute.

She missed Dawn so bad she couldn't breathe most days. They'd been inseparable since they were kids. They'd been through everything together, and now Felicity was left to manage her grief alone.

Her phone rang in her pocket, and she debated answering it. She didn't feel like talking to anyone, but it was also a distraction from the monumental task of going through Dawn's things.

Felicity would need a new roommate soon or she wouldn't be able to afford the rent.

She knew who was calling. Her brother Jameson had called every other hour for the past week.

She inhaled a deep breath and answered. "Hey." If she wanted her brother to think she was fine, the lone word sounded semi-convincing. In truth, she hadn't brushed her hair in days, and the only thing she'd eaten this week was ramen noodles.

"You okay?" Jameson asked.

"Yep." Again, another passable attempt at pretending not to be crumbling under the weight of her grief.

"I just talked to my boss. I can come by tomorrow."

She could pack up Dawn's things on her own, but she needed her brother's truck to get them to the local thrift store.

"Thanks. I'll be here."

Unfortunately, she didn't have anywhere to be for the foreseeable future. Losing her job at the lumber mill yesterday had been the icing on the cake of the world's worst week.

"You sure you're okay?" Jameson asked again. "What time do you get off work?"

Felicity stepped back and closed the bedroom door, feeling relieved that she could wait until tomorrow when Jameson showed up to tackle the memories in her cousin's room. "I got let go yesterday at work."

"You're kidding me," Jameson spat.

"Yeah. It's not like this is a shock. I knew it was coming." The lumber mill had a zero-tolerance policy for tardiness or missed attendance. There were too many people in the small town clamoring for the jobs the lumber mill provided.

"That's ridiculous. Your cousin was dying, and they expected you to work out your shift?"

"It's fine. I'll get my resume updated and start applying."

She couldn't even bring herself to care. If she could go back and do it all again, she would have still left work mid-shift when she got the call from Aunt Josie. A ripping pain slashed through Felicity's chest when she thought about that call.

She kept hoping it was all a long, cruel nightmare. She wanted to wake up and forget all about her cousin's overdose.

"Don't worry. We'll find you a new job."

Felicity rested the phone between her ear and shoulder as she turned on the kitchen sink to wash the lone bowl she'd used to eat her breakfast for one—again.

"I can find my own job, but thanks for the offer."

Jameson's huff was quiet but discernible. They both knew too much about the risk of unemployment. Without an income, things could go south fast. They'd lived it in a vicious cycle throughout their childhood.

Every time their mother had lost her job, Felicity had come up with a way to save their family. Jameson had been too young, and she couldn't watch him starve, even if their mother hadn't seemed to care.

This time, she hadn't been able to save Dawn, and all of the hard work she'd put into getting her cousin on the right track felt like a waste of time. What was the point?

"I don't like this," he said, his tone low like a warning.

"Me either." She didn't like that the rent had just doubled, she didn't like the funeral bills she'd just inherited, and she didn't like sitting in this lonely house all day and night.

She heard the roaring of a diesel engine followed by the warning barks of Boone. Her trusty Black and Tan was as good as a security alarm.

She peeked out the picture window above the sink. A familiar burgundy pickup was parked in the driveway.

Felicity groaned. "I have to go. Cain is here."

"Don't open the door for him."

"You don't have to tell me twice." Cain was her least favorite person right now, and the last person on the planet she wanted to see.

Felicity's thoughts about Dawn's on-again off-again boyfriend were anything but saintly. How could someone be so heartless? His girlfriend just died, and he'd been MIA ever since.

The front doorknob rattled, and Felicity sprinted to the door. "Gotta go. He has a key."

"Wait!"

She heard Jameson's order, but she didn't have time to wait. Cain already had the door open, but she positioned herself in the entryway to block him.

Dawn had a type—bad boys—and Cain fit the bill better than any of them. Felicity's skin prickled when he was around, and she always fought the instinct to run.

It was his eyes. They were so dark she wondered if there was any light inside him.

Felicity knew how to stand up to men. She'd been doing it at a young age when her mother let them into their home. Strangers who ate all of their food and complained about Jameson's infant cries. She'd been nine the first time she'd called the police for help, but that came after her mother's flavor of the week had backhanded her to the floor.

Felicity straightened her shoulders and steeled her voice. "What do you want?"

"I came to get some of my stuff." He stepped inside and used his shoulder to push her out of the way.

She righted herself and followed him into the house. "You've got a lot of nerve showing up here." Her control was slipping. Her anger was mounting. The injustice of Dawn's death hit her square in the chest.

He ignored her, and she followed him to Dawn's room. He knelt beside the bed and reached beneath it to pull out a shoe box.

"Stop it!" Felicity screamed.

Cain opened the box and quickly located two tiny objects. The diamond earrings Dawn had loved.

"You can't take those," Felicity seethed.

"Move." He forcefully shoved her out of his way as he stalked back through the house.

Just as he walked out the door, she set free the rage that had been building inside of her. "You killed her, and you didn't even show up to the funeral!"

Cain stopped and turned to her, the movement slow and controlled like a predator sizing up its prey. Boone barked incessantly from the fenced-in front yard, heightening the tension in the air.

Movement caught Felicity's attention, and she saw her neighbor, Fred Nix, step out onto his porch and fold his thick arms over his chest. There wasn't any love lost between Fred and Felicity, but she wanted to kiss the old coot for making an appearance if only as a witness.

When Cain looked over his shoulder to see what she was looking at behind him, she had a split-second idea and jerked his key from the lock where he'd left it. He turned back to her just as she threw it with all her might toward the thick bushes that lined Fred's property.

Felicity's heart pounded in her chest as Cain eyed the indistinct area where she'd thrown the key. She said a quick, fervent prayer knowing she'd probably sealed her fate. If she was about to meet her Maker, she wanted to be on good terms with Him.

Sure enough, Cain's mouth pursed into a tight line, and his eyes narrowed. She'd seen him mad at Dawn plenty of times, but she'd never seen *this*.

A wave of stupidity disguised as bravery washed over her, and she held his gaze as she whispered, "Choke on it."

Cain lunged at her, and she ducked. Twisting to the side, she jammed her heel into his shin and thrust her elbow up into his ribs. He stumbled at the attacks, but he was barely affected. Her one hundred and thirty pounds were nothing against his two hundred.

She didn't need to maim him, but she'd accomplished her goal of getting him out of the way. She darted back inside, slammed the door closed, and flipped the deadbolt.

Cain's fists landed heavy on the other side of the door. His curses and threats were drowned out by Boone's barking.

Felicity tucked her chin and linked her hands behind her neck as she whispered a prayer. *Calm. Peace. Lord, anything.*

Cain's poundings soon silenced, and she lifted her head to suck in a deep breath. She'd either just made a huge mistake or he'd gotten what he wanted and he'd leave her alone.

Her hand shook as she lifted it to cover her mouth. She'd tried to pull Dawn away from the people who dragged her down with them, but judging from Cain's visit, Felicity had failed miserably.

A high-pitched whistle had the hairs on her arms rising and a wave of cold dread running down her body. "No."

She flipped the dead bolt and jerked the door open. She sprinted around the house to the driveway. Small rocks and sticks jabbed the soles of her feet, but the pain was secondary to the immediate problem.

"Stop!" she screamed at the top of her lungs.

Cain had a grip on Boone's collar, and with one jerk, her dog was flung into the back seat of the pickup truck.

"No! Cain! Stop!"

He ignored her as he slid into the driver's seat, closed the door, and flung gravel as he sped out of her driveway.

"Boone!"

Felicity felt the cold sting of tears sliding over her temples as she ran after the truck. She sucked in jagged breaths through her teeth as the sobs made it impossible to continue running. She needed air. She needed the pain in her chest to go away.

Stopping at the end of the road, she braced her hands on her knees and panted.

Cain. This was all Cain's fault. He'd taken Dawn, and now he'd taken Boone. Her friends. Her family.

He'd taken everything from her.

She stood and looked around. The neighborhood was filled with old houses in various states of decline. She'd been fighting this battle with life for over thirty years now, and she was tired of merely surviving. Living paycheck to paycheck her whole life was enough to break her, and now she didn't even have that.

Was this her breaking point? Was it all going to come crashing down on her where she stood in the tall grass on the side of the road in a rundown neighborhood?

Apparently, it was, and she had no idea how to pick herself up from this one. But what choice did she have but to keep fighting? She couldn't just sit down here and wait for nothing.

No one was going to save her. She'd learned early on that she had to save herself.

The roaring of a speeding truck drew her attention, and for a moment, she worried that Cain was coming back to finish her off. Then all the tension left her shoulders when she spotted Jameson's truck.

Just this one time, she'd let Jameson save her.

The truck screeched to a halt in front of her, and Jameson jumped out.

"What are you doing? I've been calling you."

She felt numb as she shook her head. "He took Boone."

Jameson's fists tightened at his sides. His nostrils flared, and his chest rose and fell in deep waves. His jaw twitched as he bit his tongue. He'd probably go home and pound a punching bag for hours.

"I don't want to talk about it," she said as she headed toward the passenger's side of his truck. If one more thing went wrong this week, she'd scream until her throat was sore.

They didn't speak on the short drive back to her house. She didn't want to say anything. Her chest felt too heavy, and any words she could manage would be garbled.

Unfamiliar silence greeted her as she stepped out of Jameson's truck. Boone was always excited to see her, and now that small piece of happiness that she looked forward to was gone.

Once they were inside, Jameson broke the silence. "You can't stay here."

Felicity rounded on him. "I appreciate the ride, but—"

"I'm not trying to tell you what to do. You know you can't stay here. Don't be stubborn about it."

She took a deep breath and tried to clear her head. Jameson was right. She just didn't like the way it sounded more like an order.

Jameson's expression softened. "I was at work."

Felicity's eyes widened. "You didn't have to leave! I was fine." They couldn't both lose their jobs.

"I will always be here when you need me. It's us against the world, remember?"

Her throat constricted at the words. She'd said them to him hundreds of times over the years.

He stepped closer and laid a hand on her shoulder. "Fortunately, I have a boss who knows family is at the top of the priority list."

"Yeah, you've got a good one." Few people were lucky enough to work for someone who understood that life happens and it isn't always expected.

Jameson took a deep breath and squeezed her shoulder. "That's why I asked them if you could move to the ranch."

Felicity jerked her head up. Her younger brother was a good foot taller than her, but he never made her feel like he was looking down on her. "What?"

"You can't afford this place on your own. I don't like Cain or any of Dawn's friends who might just show up and cause trouble. And the Hardings always need an extra hand. The place is booming."

"I told you I could find my own job," Felicity reminded him.

"Yeah, and I found you one anyway. You can be mad about it while we pack up your things."

Her hands perched on her hips, and she leveled him with a cold stare as she prepared to argue.

He held up a hand. "Don't. I know you're more than capable. You've always taken charge, and now it's my turn. Don't turn your cheek to a good thing because of your pride."

She took three steadying breaths before she was able to truly understand what he was saying.

Jameson continued, "Cain is bad news, and he'll be back. Guys like that don't let things go."

She sighed. "I may have thrown his key into the bushes," she admitted.

Jameson let his head fall back. "Seriously? I'm glad he doesn't have a key, but you didn't do yourself any favors with that stunt."

"I know. I was just… angry. And hurt."

Her brother's arms wrapped around her, and she rested her head on his chest. Exhaustion washed over her. She was tired of always standing tall. Her life required constant vigilance, at least while she'd been living with Dawn. She'd brought trouble after trouble to their doorstep.

"I need you to come to the ranch," Jameson said. This time, there wasn't any demand in his voice, only pleading.

"No offense, but I don't want to live with you."

Jameson chuckled. "I don't want to live with you either. You're too bossy."

"It's my job."

"No, I'm a grown man, and you don't have to raise me anymore. You did just fine, but you're free now."

Free? She'd spent her teen years looking out for Jameson and her adult life trying to keep Dawn out of trouble. She felt a little lost without someone to need her.

But she wasn't free. The unrelenting bills were a reminder that she would always serve a master who signed her paycheck. Right now, she wasn't in a position to be responsible for herself, much less someone else.

She forced a smile and patted her brother on the shoulder. "You turned out pretty good."

"You don't have to live with me. There's an open cabin on the ranch."

Jameson had moved into an old cabin at Blackwater Ranch about a year ago, and he'd only ever said good things about the family he worked for. She knew the Hardings. She'd gone to school with the oldest brother, Micah. But they didn't owe her anything, and she didn't want to be in debt to anyone.

"What's the job?"

Jameson shrugged. "I didn't get that far. I was kind of in a hurry because I didn't want you here alone with Cain at the door. Probably just whatever they need help with at the moment. Haley manages the bed and breakfast, but she'll be out on maternity leave soon, so she might train you to take over some of those duties."

Felicity bit her lip and looked at the floor. She wasn't attached to this place, and she didn't have a way to afford it. A job and a place to sleep sounded like an offer she couldn't pass up.

Jameson continued, "They gave me the rest of the day off to help you."

Felicity smiled. It seemed the Lord had made a way for her when she'd been hopeless—again. "Well, we better get to work."

Chapter Two

HUNTER

Hunter slung a large bag of dog food into the cart and waited for Laney to read him the next item on the list. He didn't mind helping his cousin's wife out at the store. She didn't make it seem like the usual female shopping experience. Laney knew what she needed, and she didn't waste time browsing. He also appreciated that she didn't try to chitchat.

She struck an item from the list she held. "Hydraulic steering fluid."

Hunter led the way to the automotive section of the store, carefully avoiding eye contact with everyone he passed. The scar on his face made everyone uncomfortable, and he didn't need to see their expressions when they judged him. Everyone in town knew the jagged edges of the line down his face, but it still drew attention.

The reactions he drew from others could go one of two ways. They either avoided looking his way, afraid of the fearsome appearance of his scar and stony frown, or they watched him like a hawk, waiting for him to steal or cause trouble.

It was unwarranted. He'd never taken a thing that wasn't his, but his old man's reputation preceded him. Apparently, a thief could only beget another thief. The apple doesn't fall far from the tree sort of thing.

"I hope you know what kind we need because I don't," Laney admitted.

Hunter grabbed a bottle of the oil and placed it in the cart.

"That's it," she said as she guided the cart toward the checkout counter.

The young girl at the cash register kept her gaze on Laney or the items as she bagged them, while Kent Price, an older man who worked at Grady's Feed and Seed, wasn't subtle about watching Hunter. The guy could watch all he wanted, but Hunter didn't intend to put on a show. Well, some people considered him part of the freak show just because he existed, but that wasn't news to anyone.

They'd reached his truck with the cart when Laney laid a hand on his arm.

"Oh, I forgot something. I'll be right back."

Hunter didn't say anything. He loaded the items, returned the cart to the store, and started the truck while he waited for Laney.

He didn't have to wait long before she jogged toward the truck. She climbed in the passenger seat and thrust a bag toward him. "Here. One of your shirts got ripped in the laundry this week."

He accepted the bag and put it in the back seat. "Thanks." It wasn't Laney's fault his shirt was torn, and she knew she didn't have to buy him a new one. So saying anything other than thanks was unnecessary.

Two more things he liked about Laney. She understood him, and she did things out of pure kindness.

Someone knocked on the driver's side window of his truck, and he turned to see Kent Price glaring at him.

Hunter rolled the window down and prepared for the old coot's usual bad attitude.

"I need to see your receipt."

Laney leaned over the console. "Well, hello to you, too. How are you this afternoon?"

Her attempt to steer the confrontation into friendly territory fell on deaf ears as Kent jerked a thumb over his shoulder. "I need you to open the back too."

Hunter tightened his jaw and got out of the truck.

Laney didn't waste any time launching into her protest. "What? Why? This is crazy."

"The receipt," Kent reiterated.

Laney huffed and pulled the strip of paper from her pocket. "Does Grady know you're out here accusing shoppers of stealing?"

That would be a big no. Hunter had been coming into Grady's store since he was a boy, and the owner was one of the folks who didn't hold Hunter accountable for his dad's sins. In fact, Grady often sent Hunter home with a little something on the house. The old man always called Hunter first if he needed a hand with anything around the house or at the Feed and Seed.

Kent took his time comparing the receipt to the contents in the back of the truck. Disdain radiated from the guy. It was as if Hunter could smell it when another man was itching for a fight, and he didn't give a rip what the guy thought about him. He recognized that tension like an old friend. The hum in the air was as common as breathing.

When Kent handed the receipt back and walked away without so much as a huff, Hunter got back in and avoided Laney's glare.

"The nerve of that man," she seethed.

Hunter backed out of the parking spot and kept any comments on Kent Price to himself.

"Doesn't that bother you?" she asked, her pitch rising with her anger.

"Let it go," Hunter said.

"But it's not fair."

"So?"

"So… Ugh. It just makes me furious," she said as she crossed her arms over her chest. She knew Kent's behavior had nothing to do with her and everything to do with Hunter.

"You don't have to go to bat for me. You aren't protecting my sterling reputation. I set that on fire a long time ago."

"No, but I know what it's like to be on the outside. You look like a troublemaker when you're always fighting, even if it's someone else's battles."

"Don't sweat it." He focused on the road ahead, already putting the confrontation with Kent behind him.

Laney was still stewing. She wasn't a stranger to injustice, but she was a strong enough woman to speak her mind. Being married to Micah had helped that. Hunter remembered when Laney came to Blackwater, meek and beaten down.

"I can handle my own," Hunter reminded her.

"I know. If it doesn't kill you, it had better start running," she said, her mouth turning up on one side into a grin.

They didn't speak the rest of the drive back to the ranch. They unloaded a few things at the main house, and he waved good-bye as he took the rest to the barn before heading back into town. He didn't want Laney around for his next errand.

Parking in front of the antique store on Second Avenue, Hunter killed the engine and texted Asa. The clock on the dash read 4:55. Right on time.

Seconds later, Hunter's friend, Asa, stepped out of the antique shop followed by his eight-year-old son, Jacob.

Jacob bounded up to the truck as Hunter stepped out.

"Hey, Mr. Harding." Jacob bounced on his toes. "Can I sit in your truck?"

Jacob asked the same question every time. The kid was into cars and had been for the better part of his life. It wasn't just cars. Pretty much anything with a motor caught Jacob's attention like a moth to a flame.

"Go ahead."

Hunter turned it off and pocketed the keys before Jacob climbed in. He wasn't interested in the bells and whistles. He just wanted to pretend he was speeding on the open road.

With Jacob off to the races, Hunter greeted Asa with a handshake before handing over the white envelope. It became easier and easier to part with half his paycheck. Hunter had wondered a few times what he'd do with the money if he didn't give it away, but he couldn't think of a single thing to do with it.

Asa folded the envelope and shoved it in the front pocket of his uniform as usual. "How's the ranch?"

"Same as always." Hunter jerked his head toward the truck where Jacob puttered engine noises and mimicked squealing tires. "You gonna send him to Jade's family fun day?"

Asa watched his son with pride. "Oh, yeah. Mom'll have to take him. I'll be on the clock."

It had never bothered Hunter that Asa was a police officer. The guy was the epitome of a model citizen, serving and protecting like it was his mission in life.

The half of the town who thought Hunter was as crooked as his old man would gawk and gossip if they saw the outcast shooting the breeze with the authorities. They were two ends of the spectrum—the dark and the light.

Hunter eyed Jacob. "You ever think about getting him a vehicle?"

Asa sighed. "I'm not ready for that. I still have a few years before he drives away." Asa rubbed his jaw. "I actually just got him a four-wheeler. It's used and needs a little work. You mind if I bring it by sometime?"

"Go right ahead. You know your way to the back barn." The barn on the northwestern edge of the ranch was for maintenance, and since Asa had sold anything and everything of value to pay for his late wife's hospital bills after the car wreck that ultimately killed her, he didn't have half the tools he needed to fix a leaky sink.

"Thanks, man."

"Give me a shout when you come by, and I'll pull a wrench with you." Hunter and Asa had formed a loose friendship in high school when they had shop class together, and they'd saved each other's skins too many times to count since.

Hunter appreciated Asa's quiet friendship. That's why he'd called on Asa to keep a secret fifteen years ago. They'd been meeting here ever since to fulfill Hunter's lifelong debt. Well, it wasn't Hunter's debt, but his dad had stolen an obscene amount of money from the ranch before he disappeared, leaving a fifteen-year-old Hunter behind.

His aunt and uncle hadn't deserved any of that, so Hunter had been giving what he could back to them. At this rate, they might get back what his dad stole from them in another fifteen years.

A few people in town knew about the mountain of money Butch had run off with, so it was easy for Asa to tell them an anonymous donor wanted to help them out.

"You don't have to do this anymore," Asa said as he patted the pocket that held the money.

Hunter shook his head. Asa knew enough, but he didn't understand the whole picture. The loss of that money had been a fresh wound when Hunter had gotten the scars that covered most of his body. His aunt and uncle hadn't batted an eye when the hospital bills started rolling in for the nephew they'd inherited.

Asa's mom stepped out of the antique shop and locked the door behind her.

Hunter jerked his head toward the truck. "I gotta run. Aaron is proposing to Jade tonight."

"It's about time." Asa narrowed his eyes. "I guess that means you're the last man standing."

Hunter shook his head. "Jameson is still a wild card, but don't hold your breath for me."

Asa's expression darkened. He knew the highs and lows of tying his life to a woman. "You might still find someone."

Hunter huffed and slapped a hand on Asa's shoulder and kept his cynical thoughts to himself. Guys like Hunter didn't get a happily ever after.

They both knew no woman would ever look past the scar on his face, and it wasn't as if he had anything to offer. Half of a paycheck, not a square foot of land to his name, and an ancestry populated by sinners.

Hunter tipped his hat. "See you tomorrow."

Asa slapped the side of Hunter's truck. "Time to go, bud."

Jacob groaned as he slipped from the driver's seat. "I was winning."

Asa's mom stopped beside Hunter and squeezed his arm. "How are you?"

"Good." The same answer for the same question every time he saw her, but how could he say anything other than good things when Mrs. Scott always wore that unfailing smile all the time?

The rumble of an old engine drew Mrs. Scott's attention, and Hunter looked over his shoulder to see Kent Price slowly rolling by in his rusted truck. His gaze darted between Hunter and Asa as he frowned hard enough to bore deep ridges between his brows.

Asa lifted a hand and smiled. He kept his attention on Kent and gritted his teeth. "We'll be the talk of the town."

Hunter slid into his truck. "He already caught me at Grady's today."

"No doubt he thinks you're paying me off to look the other way while you steal his goat or kick his chickens."

Mrs. Scott hiked her purse strap higher on her shoulder. "That man has too much time on his hands."

Kent was infamous for his riotous disposition. He'd gotten the local volunteer fire department's weekly bingo game shut down on the grounds of gambling. He didn't care that the old people sat around and talked while they donated to the first responders who served the community.

He'd even been bold enough to claim it wasn't Christlike to gamble, as if Kent had ever stepped foot in a church or owned a Bible.

Asa directed Jacob toward the police car. "Don't worry about him. He's mad enough that I know about that time he got drunk and crashed a truck into Grady's house."

Mrs. Scott swatted Asa's arm. "It's not nice to speak ill of someone," she reprimanded.

"What? It's funny. Someone should start a petition to suspend his license."

Hunter rolled his eyes. He'd seen half a dozen of Kent's alleged petitions. Each was more ridiculous than the last.

Jacob raised his hand. "I signed the one about longer lunch breaks."

Asa squinted at his son. "You don't even work at Grady's. And who let you sign that?"

Mrs. Scott rolled her eyes. "It was the silliest thing I'd ever heard, and I knew Grady would get a laugh out of it."

Asa laid a hand on Jacob's shoulder. "Get in the car. I have a few things to talk to Granny about on the way home."

Asa slid into the driver's seat of the patrol car with a lift of his chin.

Hunter's part of the deal had been taken care of, and Asa would pass the anonymous donation along to Silas Harding tomorrow after church.

Mrs. Scott grabbed Hunter's truck door as he reached to close it. Her grin squinted her eyes and lifted the mounds of her cheeks. "You know Kent is wrong. He's not like everyone else."

Hunter nodded. "I know, but I'm not like everyone else either."

Mrs. Scott rested a gentle hand on his arm. She reminded him so much of his Aunt Anita. Always kind and looking out for kids who weren't her own.

But Hunter wasn't a kid anymore, and he liked it that she didn't know about half the injustices he lived with every day.

"He never liked Butch," she reminded Hunter.

It was still odd to hear the name. He couldn't even put a face with the man in his memories anymore. "Not many people did."

"And with good reason, but that has nothing to do with you."

"I know, Mrs. Scott."

She patted his arm before pulling away. "You do enough good for this town. I don't know why everybody can't see it."

Mrs. Scott was on the hospitality committee at the church, and she knew he would leave here and drive straight to the church to cut the grass, just like always.

Hunter tightened his jaw and studied the large window of the antique shop. "I don't want everybody to see it. I'm allergic to pomp and circumstance."

Mrs. Scott gave him a friendly wink and backed away from the truck. "You take care. I'll see you in the morning."

Chapter Three

FELICITY

The fifteen-minute drive to Blackwater Ranch felt like an eternity. The weight of the boxes packed in the trunk, back seat, and passenger seat of her old Corolla might as well have been on her shoulders.

Was moving out a good idea? What if she was just leaving the place to be taken over by Cain? He didn't have a key anymore, but he probably wasn't above breaking and entering.

The one box she didn't want to think about sat beside her with "Boone" scrawled across it. Her throat tightened when she thought about her dog. Did Cain keep him or drop him off on the side of the road somewhere? Was he being fed?

With a deep breath, she reminded herself that Boone was a coon dog. He could survive if

Cain had thrown him out. She almost preferred that option to the thought of Boone being subjected to Cain and his twisted mind. Nothing around that man was safe.

Her cell phone rang, and she answered when she saw it was Aunt Josie.

"Hello."

"Felicity?" Aunt Josie was already breathing hard. "I just stopped by the house, and you aren't home."

Anything out of the ordinary triggered Aunt Josie's anxiety. Her attacks had been frequent before her daughter's death, but she lived in a constant state of panic now.

Felicity took a second to adopt her most calming voice. "Do you remember that I told you Cain came by yesterday? He was really hostile, and Jameson suggested I stay at Blackwater Ranch for a while."

"You think he's that dangerous?" Aunt Josie squealed.

Felicity debated. If she told the truth, her aunt would no doubt spin into a panic attack, and she'd have to turn around and make sure she used her inhaler before following her home.

"I don't know. I think it's better safe than sorry. I also don't think I can keep paying the rent on that place without Dawn." Felicity decided against disclosing her current unemployment status. She often had to help her Aunt Josie pay her bills, and that was another thing that would push her over the edge.

"Oh, goodness. Me too, baby girl. I don't know how I can go on without her."

Aunt Josie's waterworks began. She cried constantly, and Felicity tried to ease the conversation into safer territory.

"I have some good news. I think I got a new job." She hadn't actually talked to her new employer, so she hoped Jameson hadn't been embellishing the job offer.

Aunt Josie sniffled. "What? What was wrong with your old one?"

"Nothing. Jameson just said that they might have an opening at the ranch, and since I'll be living there, it'll be much easier to get to work." She'd been stacking items in the pro column for this job since she'd talked it over with Jameson yesterday. Less mileage and no rent payment were at the top of the list.

"Oh, that does sound good," Aunt Josie agreed. Her hysterical tone softened. "I guess I'll just head on then."

"Did you need something? You can visit me at the ranch if you'd like, or I can swing by in the evenings." Inviting her aunt to the new place sounded less like a warning to stay away from the old house and more like a welcoming suggestion.

"I was just out visiting. I'll run by Trudy's and see what she's up to."

Visiting is what Aunt Josie did, and she treated it like a job. She'd been receiving a disability check from the government since a gas leak at the plant where she'd worked had left her with permanent lung damage in her thirties.

Felicity's phone buzzed against her ear, and she pulled it away to see her brother's name on the screen.

She jumped back to the call with Aunt Josie. "That sounds like a good idea. I'll talk to you soon."

"Bye," Aunt Josie sang.

Felicity accepted the call from Jameson. "Hey, I'm almost there."

Her thoughts on the new move were still confusing, and Jameson had called her twice since he left her house yesterday. It felt a lot like her brother was checking up on her, and there were few things she disliked more than being coddled. He was still her little brother, even if he had a foot of height advantage.

"Sorry, but something came up. I won't be there until later, but I'm about to call Hunter and see if he can show you where your cabin is."

"Hunter Harding?" She'd known *of* him in high school, but she didn't know much about him besides what the whole town knew: his dad was a crook.

She also knew about the scar on his face. He'd gotten it sometime while they were still in school, and the rumors ranged from bad to worse. Some said he'd been attacked by a bear and won. Others claimed his dad was to blame.

Felicity didn't know what to believe, and she really didn't want to know. She'd seen him a few times in town, and the man had a way of warding people off with a dark glare. She resolutely wanted no part of it.

"Thanks. I'll find it."

"I know. Laney and Anita will come by later to explain your job duties."

"Okay."

An awkward silence fell on the call as if Jameson wasn't finished speaking. Then he sighed and said, "I'm really glad you got out of there. I know you don't really want to do this, but I think it's gonna be great for you. The Hardings are like my family."

She gasped and immediately hoped Jameson hadn't heard her reaction.

"Not that you haven't been great," he continued. "It's nothing against you. I just like that they look after each other. It's like what you and I do, but there are more of them. You'll see."

Felicity wasn't sure what to say. She wanted to have that hope, but it was hard to look on the bright side when she was sitting at rock bottom. "Thanks."

"The Hardings are good folks. You'll see."

She slowed to turn at the hanging Blackwater Ranch sign. "I'm here. I'll see you later."

"Yeah. I'll stop by when I get back. And I've been praying for you." He added the last part with a resolute tone she hadn't heard before.

If she'd done one thing right, it was take her brother to church. Her first boss had encouraged her to attend, and she and Jameson had both clung to the continuous hope of the church. They'd never had a dad, but it was comforting to know they had someone watching over them.

Granted, sometimes she wished God would intervene on her behalf just a little. She'd heard all about blessings, but it had always felt like she and Jameson were stuck in a generational curse. Felicity still didn't have the hang of the religion thing, but she hoped one day she'd figure out how it all worked. She really wanted on God's good side.

"Thanks. I need it." If there was ever a time for praying, it was now.

"Plus, I may get to see you more often. We have breakfast, lunch, and dinner at the main house together."

"Every day?" Felicity asked as she eased down the drive leading into the ranch.

"Yep. I gotta run. See you later."

"Bye."

She tossed the phone in the passenger seat and studied the ranch. The entire landscape was beautiful. The drive led straight to an enormous wooden house surrounded by cars and trucks. The field to her left was wide open as far as the eye could see with only a far-away barn sitting atop a distant rise.

Just before the large house, the road diverged to either side. When she looked to her right, she could see a row of cabins nestled against the tree line in a slight depression, and she changed course. One of them must be her new place.

As she approached, she steered toward the only vehicle in sight—a black pickup truck parked in front of one of the farther cabins. When she was close enough to distinguish the outline of the man standing beside the truck, she knew she'd found Hunter, and he didn't look happy to see her.

She wasn't scared of any man. She'd stood her ground in front of Cain and all the vile men who'd tried to beat her down before him, but the imposing frame of Hunter Harding caused a reaction within her that she couldn't quite place. Was it nervousness?

She parked beside the black truck and got out. Her goal was to get inside and shut away from everyone before the heavy tears decided to break free.

Hefting her bulging suitcase from the trunk, she put off acknowledging Hunter's presence as long as she could.

When he reached for her bag, she pulled it closer. She needed to be capable of handling something on her own, and carrying her own bag was where she intended to start. "Which one?"

He pointed, and her attention followed the direction he indicated. The traitorous tears flooded her eyes until everything turned blurry.

She closed the trunk and stalked toward the cabin. Hopefully, Hunter would get the message that she didn't want his help right now. If she had to actually tell him, the waterworks would begin.

Once inside, she rested her back against the old wooden door and let the tears fall. If she purged the pesky moisture, she'd be able to pick herself up and get to work. Right now, she couldn't even make out what her new home looked like. The sobs racked her body, and she covered her mouth to silence the whine that escaped.

For the first time in her life, no one was depending on her. Jameson was grown, and she'd failed Dawn miserably. While she'd always wondered what it would feel like to be free to live her own life, the moment itself came with a hollow sense of uselessness.

Chapter Four

HUNTER

Hunter added his empty breakfast plate to the top of the stack of other discarded plates on the end of the serving bar. The few couples who were guests at the bed and breakfast were slowly clearing out, and he stayed behind to help Anita clean up.

He tried to offer at least once a week. There were times during the spring and summer seasons when he didn't get the chance, but he didn't want Anita to think he'd forgotten her. He owed her a debt he'd never be able to repay, so he washed dishes and cleaned tables without complaining.

In the kitchen, Anita already had her hands in soapy water up to her elbows in the sink, so he left the dirty dishes on the counter and grabbed a broom.

"Oh, could you do something for me? Jameson said his sister would be here for breakfast this morning, but I didn't see her. Would you mind taking her a plate and checking in?"

Hunter contemplated his options. He'd never refused anything his aunt had asked of him, but for some reason, he didn't want to get caught up with Felicity.

Seconds ticked by as Hunter ground his teeth trying to think of a way out of paying Felicity a visit, but every time he thought of turning down his aunt, he remembered that she'd never once forgotten him. Hunter wasn't her son, but she hadn't treated him any different than her own flesh and blood.

Before he made up his mind, Anita jerked her head toward the pantry. "To-go containers are on the top shelf. Don't be stingy. She didn't come by for supper last night either."

It seemed like he had less say in the request than he thought.

"Yes, ma'am." He put the broom down and grabbed two boxes from the pantry.

Without knowing what Felicity would like, he added some of everything to the boxes before grabbing plasticware and napkins. He'd heard her make a few trips out to her car the night before, but she hadn't left the ranch. There was a good chance she didn't have much moved in yet if she'd only moved one carload in.

Minutes later, he parked his truck in front of her house. The nearness to his own had the hairs on the back of his neck standing up. Laney hadn't bothered him when she'd lived there before she married his cousin, Micah, but Felicity's disruption of his solitude remained to be seen.

Dixie perked her head up as he stepped out of the truck. The border collie was always hanging around someone's feet, and Hunter wasn't a fan of her attention.

The dog must have smelled the food because she stood and tilted her nose toward the boxes.

"This isn't for you," Hunter said, lifting the boxes higher.

Dixie either didn't care or didn't understand because she paced from his left side to his right and back again.

Hunter ignored Dixie as he knocked on the door. Soft rustling sounded from inside, and Felicity opened the door seconds later.

He recalled her general features from high school, but being this close was like getting a peek under a microscope. Her brown hair was pulled back in a tight ponytail, and she wore a plain gray shirt and tight black pants. He tried not to let his focus linger on the material that hugged the curves of her lower half, but that left him scrambling for something else to focus on.

When she looked up at him, her gaze locked with his, and those amber eyes captured his attention.

Yesterday, Hunter could have said with all honesty that he'd never been entranced by a woman. Today, he wasn't so sure. Curiosity got the better of him, and he wondered if that was sadness or irritation he saw in her eyes.

She tucked her arms around her middle and straightened, lifting her chin slightly. "Hi."

Suddenly, the unnamed look that had drawn him in was gone, replaced by apprehension.

"Anita sent breakfast." He held out the containers, making sure to note that the package wasn't from him. He didn't want Felicity getting things twisted between them.

She accepted the boxes. "Thanks."

Hunter tipped his hat. "I'm just the delivery boy." He severed any trance he'd been wrangled in and turned to go.

"Hey," Felicity said from behind him.

He stopped, turned, and waited for her to ask something else of him. Apparently, he was the welcoming committee at Blackwater Ranch these days.

"Sorry about yesterday. I wasn't my best self."

He wasn't sure what he'd expected, but it wasn't an apology.

"I won't bother you," she added.

He nodded, accepting her silent treaty, before turning to go.

"You don't like me very much," she said.

Here we go. Why did she care if he liked her? It didn't make much of a difference. He hadn't actually said if he did or didn't like her. He hadn't given it much thought either.

He turned and tried to ignore the look of exhaustion and defeat on her face. "Don't take it personally. I don't like myself either."

Felicity pointed at Dixie, who was still hanging around Hunter's feet, even after he'd given up the food. "She likes you."

Hunter eyed the dog. The only problem he had with Dixie was that she didn't leave well enough alone. She was the animal equivalent of the stereotypical peppy cheerleader who walked through life as if it were a series of rainbows and unicorns.

"She just won't give up," Hunter said.

"You don't like dogs?" Felicity questioned.

He knew the answer she was looking for. Her tone said it all.

Hunter shrugged. "I don't like anyone."

That answer softened her scowl, and a look of recognition took its place. "Me either." She looked back to Dixie. "There must be some reason why she likes you."

"If you figure it out, let me know." He turned and headed for the truck with Dixie on his heels.

Felicity watched him from the porch with the boxes in her hands. Dixie returned to her place on the porch, taking up watch beside the new resident. Everyone watched him. Why did he feel seen and not accused when Felicity looked at him?

Something about the short conversation with Felicity felt different. Was it her apology? It hadn't been necessary.

No, that wasn't it. He turned his truck toward the main house and his heel tapped rapidly on the floorboard. What was it?

When he parked, the children's events coordinator, Jade, was standing on the porch with a couple and their son.

Hunter stepped out of the truck as she gestured toward the play area beside the main house. Jade was focused on the plan she had to keep the kids active and learning, but the couple was focused on him.

Everything clicked into place. In the few moments he'd spent with Felicity, she had kept eye contact. She hadn't stared at his scar.

And for once, he'd been more than just the man behind the scar.

Chapter Five

FELICITY

Felicity tore the tape on another box and heard the front door open. Who was she kidding? There was only one door.

Scrambling to her feet from the bedroom floor, she peeked into the living room to see Jameson hanging his hat on the wall by the entrance.

"Hey. You settling in okay?"

"Yeah. Everything is fine." She wasn't really sure if everything was fine. Everything was *different*, and maybe that's what made her nervous more than anything.

"Mama Harding said you didn't come to breakfast." He sniffed and eyed the half-eaten plates of food on the table. "Looks like she brought it to you. Did you already talk about the job?"

"Hunter dropped it off. I didn't feel like going to breakfast, and you said Anita wouldn't have time to meet with me until later in the morning. Is Mama Harding Anita? I can't keep the names straight."

Jameson's eyes widened. "Hunter brought you breakfast?" he asked, seeming more enthralled by the idea than answering her question about names.

"Yeah. Is that bad?" He'd seemed reluctant and maybe put out with the errand, but that may have had more to do with her rudeness yesterday when she showed up.

"Not bad. Just surprising. He's not very friendly."

"I noticed."

Jameson scratched the back of his head. His indistinct brown hair that matched hers was rumpled. "I know I said I could help you clean some stuff out today, but I just got called in at the fire station. That's why I stopped by."

Felicity waved a hand. "It's fine. I can go by myself."

"I'd rather you didn't. I can see if one of the other guys can go with you."

Felicity's shoulders hunched in a little, and she worked to straighten her spine. She didn't love the idea of being stuck with a stranger for hours. "I'm really okay by myself."

Jameson laid a hand on her shoulder. "I can't help it if I worry about you."

Felicity grinned. "That's my job—worrying about you."

"Not anymore."

She was proud of the way Jameson had turned out, and she couldn't ask for a better brother. "I want to be able to go to my house by myself."

"I know. This whole thing is messed up, but I don't trust Cain as far as I can throw him. He's one of those guys who thinks he's above the law, and that doesn't sit well with me when you're involved."

That momentary freedom she'd imagined yesterday wasn't really hers yet, but she needed to get as much done today as she could before she reported for the first day of her new job. "I get it. Thanks, but I'll be okay."

Eager to change the subject, Jameson pointed toward the door. "Looks like you got a new friend out there."

Thinking about the dog that had showed up on her porch this morning caused an ache in her chest. "Yeah, she's been hanging around. What's her name?" She desperately tried to hide the shake in her voice. The black-and-white border collie looked nothing like Boone, but it was a reminder that she missed *her* dog.

"Dixie. She's not Boone, but she's a good one too."

Felicity bit her lips between her teeth and nodded.

"Please don't cry. We'll find him."

Jameson wrapped her in a hug, and she stopped breathing as she tried as hard as she could to restrain the tears.

After a moment, he whispered, "You'll like Dixie too. Give her a chance."

Felicity knew she would like Dixie. It wasn't her fault that she dredged up painful memories. "I know."

Jameson pulled out of the embrace. "I hate it, but I have to go. I'm not sure what time, but Anita said she'd come get you and take you up to the main house this morning to show you around. You're included in all meals. Breakfast is early, but lunch is at noon, and supper is at 6:30 or so. I probably won't see you for a couple of days. I don't know how long they'll need me at the fire station."

Felicity crossed her arms over her chest. "It's fine. I've got plenty to keep me busy."

Jameson picked up his hat and rested it on his head. "See ya, sis."

With her brother gone, Felicity got back to work. She peeked inside every closet, cabinet, and drawer. The place was pretty tidy, despite its apparent age. Jameson said another woman had lived here last year. Why didn't she live here anymore?

Close to an hour later, Felicity jumped as a knock on the door startled her. She stepped from the bathroom where she'd been unpacking. "Coming!"

She opened the front door to find two smiling women waiting on the small cabin porch. One was older with her graying hair tied back in a clip, while the other was beaming with youth that matched the radiance of her dark-blonde hair and green eyes.

"Hey, I'm Laney," the younger woman said as she stuck out a hand. The other held a thin folder.

"I'm Anita," the other said, "but you can call me Mama Harding." She stepped forward with her arms open wide.

"Oh," Felicity said, startled by the forward greeting. She didn't consider herself a hugger, but apparently Mama Harding was one.

"We're so glad you're here," Mama Harding said.

"Really?" Why would they be so excited for her arrival?

"Jameson talks about you all the time," Laney said.

Felicity tilted her head. Did he? She hadn't been spending as much time with him lately because of Dawn's spiral, and Felicity felt a twinge of guilt.

"Are you settling in okay?" Laney asked.

Felicity slapped a hand on her forehead. "Where are my manners? Come in." She moved to allow the women through the door. "I guess I haven't gotten used to the idea of living here."

Laney pulled a chair from the kitchen table and sat. "You'll get used to it quickly. You know, this used to be my place. I kinda miss it."

"Oh, I didn't know." So that explained what happened to the previous tenant.

"I moved in with Micah when we got married. We're talking about building a bigger place on the ranch, but we haven't decided on a house plan yet."

"Um, can I get you something to drink?" Felicity asked, hoping they didn't want anything fancier than tap water.

"I'm fine," Mama Harding stated as she took a seat at the table.

"Me too," Laney said.

"Okay, then." Felicity sat and rested her linked hands in her lap.

Mama Harding rubbed a hand on Felicity's shoulder. "We're so glad you're here. You're welcome to stay as long as you like. Housing is included as part of your job, but there isn't TV. We do have the internet here now. Your meals are included too. Unfortunately, the pay isn't much."

"That's okay. I don't need much more than food and a place to sleep."

Laney slid a page over the table toward Felicity. "Here are the specifics. You won't have any utility bills here. I do the laundry at the main house, so everyone just drops their laundry off at the back door of the main house. I bring it back when it's clean."

"This is so much." Well, the pay wasn't much, but it felt like the Hardings were getting the short end of the stick. She scanned the job duties. There wasn't anything on the list she couldn't handle.

"Haley is the manager of the bed and breakfast, and she'll be out on maternity leave soon. Since I manage the ranch outside of the bed and breakfast, I don't really want to take on those duties as well. It's a lot. Plus, I'm the housekeeper for the bed and breakfast, as well as the main house, so I have a lot on my plate."

"I see," Felicity whispered as she studied the paperwork. There was more to the ranch than meets the eye.

"You'll mostly be shadowing Haley until it's time for the baby. The day starts at 8:00 every morning or after breakfast. You'll have one day off each week, but we'd like it if you didn't choose Friday or Saturday. Haley takes off on Friday, and Saturday is a busy day for check-ins and checkouts."

"I can do that. I don't really have a preference," Felicity said.

Laney rested her hand on the folder. "We can sign the paperwork now, or you can have some time to think about it and read it over."

"I can sign now. I definitely want the job."

Mama Harding handed Felicity a pen, and she signed wherever Laney indicated.

"Looks like we're all done." Laney straightened the papers in the folder. "Do you want a tour now?"

"Sure." The few remaining boxes could wait to be unpacked until later.

Felicity followed the ladies outside. The minivan waiting in front of the cabin was a surprise.

Laney took her place in the driver's seat, and Mama Harding gestured for Felicity to take the front passenger seat.

"This is Jade's minivan," Laney said as she buckled her seatbelt. "She let us borrow it so we could have more room as we ride around the ranch. Jade is the children's activities coordinator. You'll love her."

Another name to remember. Learning a new job wasn't new to Felicity, but the learning period was always stressful. The barrage of information thrown at her was always difficult to manage.

"Do you think we should start at the stables, Mama?" Laney asked.

Mama Harding hummed her approval. "That sounds perfect."

Stables? "Um, do I have to do anything with the horses?" Felicity asked.

"Oh, no. Lucas and Maddie have them handled," Mama Harding said.

"I... um," Felicity stammered. "I don't like horses."

Laney's eyes widened. "Oh, well, we can skip that part of the tour then. I'll just drive by the stables so you'll know where it is."

Felicity released a strained breath. She didn't flat-out dislike horses, but they were a bit scary. They seemed too powerful and wild, and anything that unpredictable gave her reason to keep her distance.

Laney pointed out the window. "There it is." She waved. "Bye, horses."

Mama Harding leaned forward from the back seat. "You can meet Lucas and Maddie later, but you won't have to be around the horses at all."

"Thanks," Felicity whispered.

"On to the north barn then," Laney said, pointing straight ahead.

Felicity couldn't see a barn if Laney had been pointing at it. There seemed to be miles of open land on every side. If all of this was the ranch, she might never leave the area with the main house and cabins for fear of getting lost.

After an hour of pointing out landmark buildings and indicating the direction of farther places on the ranch, Laney and Mama Harding returned Felicity to her cabin.

Laney got out too and followed Felicity to the porch. "I'll get your laundry now if you have any. Then you won't have to drag it up later."

"Oh, I appreciate that, but I hate to put that on you. I can wash my own laundry."

"It's no problem! Camille, Noah, Asher, and Haley all have their own houses now and do their own, so I have a lighter load these days anyway."

"I was actually about to make a trip into town for a few things. I'll just run by the laundromat."

"Suit yourself. We need to get back to the main house to serve lunch. You coming?"

Laney's question had an eager tone, but Felicity wasn't ready to jump into the community meals just yet. "I was thinking about grabbing something in town."

"Okay, then. Haley should be around tomorrow to start showing you around. Be at the main house around seven for breakfast or eight to start work."

"Thanks. I'll see you later." Felicity waved and tried to hold her grin. Meeting new people was nerve-racking, but she was even tenser because she really wanted these people to like her. So far, she was hanging on by a thread, and her attempts to be friendly were severely overshadowed by Laney and Mama Harding's sunny dispositions.

Felicity had never been the sweetest, but she wasn't unkind either. She'd just been beaten down and a little jaded by her early years, and friendship seemed like a lot of work.

Things would get easier here. She was still feeling the shock of Dawn's death and missing Boone.

Felicity loaded her laundry into her car and drove to the laundromat. The place was quiet, and she had a long wait ahead of her. She filled the washers and turned on the machines.

Taking a seat by the window facing Second Street in the heart of Blackwater, she felt an itchy unease. What would she do while she waited?

She pulled her phone from her pocket and texted Jameson.

Felicity: I'm running some errands in town, then I'm going by the house to pack up some stuff.

Jameson's reply was quick.

Jameson: Be careful. Call me if you need anything.

Hopefully, she wouldn't be calling him. When had she turned into the woman who couldn't run errands and visit her own house without a bodyguard? The confrontation with Cain had shaken her up, and she was closer to accepting her brother's help than she cared to admit.

When her laundry was finished and she'd decided that Laney probably needed a raise if she washed laundry for half the ranch workers, Felicity made her way to the end of the block toward Hanover Road where she'd parked. She watched the cars pass up and down the street. She wasn't a stranger to watching out for trouble, and she didn't want another run-in with Cain, even in public.

She reached the car and shifted the hamper to her hip while she rummaged for the keys in her purse. When she pulled them out, she lost her grip and they hit the ground with a jingle.

Bending to get them, Felicity's attention fell on the tire in front of her, and she gasped. The rubber of the tire was gashed wide open, and the rim sat heavy on the asphalt.

She stood and turned in a circle, surveying the sidewalks and nearby storefronts. Did Cain do this? Did he know she was here?

Grabbing the keys, she unlocked the door and threw the laundry in the back seat. She looked left and right, back and forth, as she popped the trunk. Jameson had taught her how to change a tire when he was in high school, but she'd only had to do it by herself once before.

It wouldn't take long, but the minutes seemed to stretch on. She was too busy watching her surroundings to give her full attention to the tire.

Fifteen minutes later, she had the spare on and the jack back in the trunk. There was still no sign of Cain or anyone who might have purposely slashed her tire, but her hands shook until she gripped the steering wheel to drive back to the ranch.

Chapter Six

HUNTER

Hunter watched Felicity where she sat with Jameson during supper. The women tried to engage with her for the first ten minutes or so before getting the hint that she wasn't comfortable answering questions.

The apples of her cheeks stayed a light shade of red throughout the meal. Jameson leaned over to whisper to her a few times, and she always nodded and mouthed "I'm okay."

A few people had already gotten up from the table when Hunter heard Felicity ask Jameson, "Since you got called off at the station, can you go with me to grab some stuff from my house? I start work tomorrow, and I want to get a few things out."

From the look on Jameson's face, Hunter could tell her brother was about to turn her down.

"I promised I'd help Bobby Green get ready for his CPAT test. He wants to be a firefighter. I told him I'd be over after supper. I completely forgot I was supposed to help you."

"It's fine." Felicity's smile fell, but only slightly.

Jameson might not have noticed, but Hunter did.

Jameson shouted over the table to Noah, "Hey, you busy right now?"

Noah's glance cut toward his wife, Camille, who looked paler than usual. She was only four months pregnant, but it seemed as if she had a new symptom every day.

"Millie isn't feeling too well. I wanted to get her settled in at the house. What do you need?"

Hunter stood and picked up his empty plate. "I'll take her."

Felicity and Jameson both whipped their attention to him. While Jameson's expression was stern and wary, Felicity's softened.

"You sure?" Jameson asked.

Felicity held up her hands. "I can really go by myself. It's fine."

She might have said it was fine, but he wasn't sure if the tension that gripped her shoulders was because of his offer or her wariness of picking up her stuff.

Jameson's brow furrowed. "I don't like you being there by yourself after what happened with Cain. I'll call Bobby and tell him I can't meet him."

"No!" Felicity said resolutely. "It's really okay."

Hunter had no idea what had happened with Cain, but he didn't like the way Jameson made it sound. If it was Cain Jenkins, it could only be bad or worse. The guy had a reputation as a seasoned criminal.

Felicity chewed her bottom lip and looked up at Hunter. Again, she didn't look scared as much as uncertain.

"Are you sure you don't mind?" she asked.

Hunter nodded. He wouldn't have offered if he didn't mean it.

Finally, she nodded. "Okay. Thanks."

Hunter headed toward the door. "I'll be outside."

Grabbing his hat on the way out, he stepped onto the porch and slid his feet into his dirty boots.

He generally didn't care if people were uncomfortable around him either because of his scar or his lack of cheery disposition, but tonight, he didn't want Felicity to worry while she was around him. Jameson said she was going through a rough patch, and Hunter hadn't seen anything north of sadness in her eyes.

Leaning against the porch railing, he looked out over the ranch. Home was a good place, but he hadn't been able to shake the nagging idea that this wasn't his home. If his dad had kept his act together, it would've all been his one day— name on the deed and everything.

But his dad had stripped him of his birthright, and now he was allowed to live and work here without even a mailbox with his name on it.

He couldn't complain. His uncle, Silas, deserved the ranch much more than Hunter's dad, Butch, who had thought running off with more than his fair share was the best way to get what he wanted.

Sounded like Butch hadn't wanted the ranch anyway. Just the money.

Hunter scanned the cars and trucks parked in front of the main house. The sun was setting, and there were only a few minutes of light left. Felicity's gray car did anything except stand out, but it caught his attention. More specifically, the spare tire on the back driver's side.

The door opened behind him, and he knew it was Felicity. Her footfalls weren't loud enough to be one of his cousins' and too purposeful to be a guest's. They tended to walk on eggshells around him.

Hunter pointed to her car. "What happened to your tire?"

Felicity rubbed the side of her head. "I had a flat earlier today."

"We should get you a new one. It's not safe to drive on the spare for too long."

Her hands rose to her hips, and her brows furrowed. The lift of her chin suggested he tread lightly.

"I can take care of that myself," she said resolutely.

"You could. Or I could call my friend, and we could drop it off at the garage tonight." He looked out toward the setting sun. "It's closed, but at least he could get to it first thing in the morning."

The rod that had held her spine straight wilted. "Okay. That sounds like a good idea. You think I could get a used one?"

"I'm sure Beau can manage that."

"I'll just follow you."

Hunter made his way to his truck, and Felicity went to her car. He waited until she was settled to start the engine and pull out. Thankfully, Beau's garage wasn't far.

Felicity parked beside Hunter in the gravel lot in front of Lawrence Tire. They both stepped out of their vehicles, and he called Beau.

Beau answered on the fourth ring. "Hello."

"Hey, Jameson's sister needs a tire. Can you get to it in the morning?"

Felicity crossed her arms over her chest. "I have a name."

Hunter huffed. He barely ever spoke, and that meant he stuck his foot in his mouth the majority of the time it was open.

"Sure thing. New or used?"

"Used if you can. Her name is Felicity." Hopefully, he could mend that one mistake and get her to stop frowning at him.

"Just put the key in the lock box by the office."

"Thanks." He ended the call and pointed to the square metal box attached to the building beside a door. "Beau said put the key in the box."

"So, I just leave it here until tomorrow?" she asked.

"Yeah. He'll call me when it's ready, and someone can bring you back to pick it up." He didn't want to volunteer himself just yet. He needed to see how she felt about riding with him first.

"Okay." She walked over and put the key in the box.

Hunter led the way to his truck and opened the passenger door for her. Uncle Silas had always told him to open doors for ladies, but this was one of the few times he'd done it for anyone except his aunt, the ladies at church, and his cousins' wives.

Felicity looked at him with wide eyes, but she climbed into the truck without comment. This might be the only time he got to hold the door for an unmarried woman, and he wasn't about to miss his chance.

Closing the door behind her, he walked around and took his place behind the wheel. Before starting the truck, he snuck a glance at Felicity and caught her looking back at him. She quickly darted her gaze away, but the look he'd seen in that split second hadn't been the same look others gave him. It was lacking the nervous curiosity that resembled a frown.

Starting the truck, he decided not to look at her again. Mostly because he *wanted* to look at her, and that wasn't a good sign. Guys like him didn't get the girl, and he knew how to stay in his lane.

She pointed out a few turns before the cab filled with silence. Twilight was in full swing, and he was acutely aware of the woman sitting beside him as he tried to keep his attention on the road illuminated by his headlights.

After a few minutes, he cleared his throat and asked the question that had been burning in his mind since supper. "You want to tell me what happened with Cain?"

Felicity's shoulders tensed. "He… Well, he was my cousin's on-again, off-again boyfriend before she died. She lived with me." She paused and looked down at her hands in her lap. "He came by to get some of *his* things the other day and left with Dawn's diamond earrings." Felicity scoffed. "I said and did some things that made him mad, and I slammed the door in his face."

Hunter rubbed his jaw. Cain's bad side was the one place no one wanted to end up. "How mad?"

"I yelled a little. And threw his key in the bushes."

Now it was Hunter's turn to tense. "You have a death wish?"

"No, but I was upset about Dawn," Felicity said, waving her hands in the air. "She was doing so well until he came back around. He always brought the drugs back. Always. If he'd stayed away, she wouldn't have gotten back on them. She'd have stayed clean. She'd still be alive."

Hunter didn't know what to say, but the shake in Felicity's voice had his fingers itching to reach for her.

But he wasn't the kind of comfort she needed.

"I'm sorry about your cousin. Jameson mentioned what happened."

Felicity pointed out another turn, and her entire demeanor had sagged as if she were exhausted. "It's the third drive on the right."

He parked in front of the indistinct white house. The front yard was fenced in, but there wasn't a dog in sight.

When he killed the engine, she looked at him, and he lost the battle with his senses as he looked back.

"I failed her," she whispered.

Hunter shook his head. "Some people can't be fixed, and that isn't your fault."

She huffed. "It still feels like it. Sometimes, I wonder if I'm the one who's broken."

Hunter frowned. "Who said you need fixing?" The question came out harsher than he'd intended.

A dog barked, and her chin lifted as she looked for the source of the noise. Spotting a full-grown pit bull a few yards down, she sighed. "I don't think Cain will come back, but thanks for coming with me." She reached for the door handle and opened it. "I'll work fast. You probably have to be up early for work in the morning."

He did have to be up at dawn, but he didn't see any point in rushing Felicity tonight. He hadn't realized she'd been living with her cousin when she died, and cleaning out the house might be more of a job than he expected.

Felicity looked over her shoulder before inserting her key into the lock. Satisfied that no danger was lurking, she opened the door and waited eagerly for Hunter to enter behind her before closing it again.

"You can make yourself at home. There isn't much except water in the fridge, but you're welcome to it."

She went to a nearby closet and started pulling sacks and bags from the top shelf. Once she'd pulled them all down, she gathered them into her arms and stalked to the kitchen.

Hunter watched from a safe distance as she knelt on the kitchen floor and began pulling open the cabinets and shoving the contents into the bags.

When she'd filled four bags, she stood with the remaining bags and walked toward the hallway. "I'll just grab some stuff from my room, and we can go."

Suddenly, she halted as if her feet were cemented to the floor. She didn't speak—just stood staring.

He didn't know what was wrong, but Felicity's change had him straightening and scanning the room.

"Felicity?"

"Someone has been here."

He looked around, but there were no signs of a disturbance. "How do you know?"

She pointed to a half open bedroom door. "That's Dawn's room. I keep the door closed because I don't want to see it. Someone opened it."

Hunter closed the space between them, giving in to the urge to be near her. "How sure are you?"

She didn't look away from the room. "Completely."

The pulse of blue lights shone through the kitchen window, and they looked at each other. The fear in her eyes lit a fire inside him, and he took another step toward her.

"Did you call the police?" he asked.

"No. Maybe there's something going on at the neighbor's."

Someone knocked at the door, but it lacked the force or urgency he expected.

Felicity pulled from her statuesque trance and moved to answer it. Hunter stayed close behind her. If there was trouble, he wanted to be by her side.

She opened it, and Hunter released the fists he'd been clenching when he saw Asa in his uniform.

Hunter's friend didn't look too surprised to see him.

"Hey, Felicity. We got a call about a strange vehicle in the drive." Asa turned to Hunter. "I didn't expect to be running a call on either of you tonight."

"Hunter came with me to get some of my things. I'm staying at Blackwater Ranch now." She twisted her finger. "Jameson was busy."

Asa held up his hands. "You don't owe me an explanation. I didn't know this was your place. Sorry to hear about Dawn."

"Thanks. I appreciated you and your mom coming to the funeral. She didn't have many people she could count on."

Everybody knew everybody in a small town. Jameson, Asa, and Hunter had been attending the same church for years, and Felicity had been close enough to Hunter and Asa's age in school that they'd crossed paths a time or two.

"Apparently, one of your neighbors is looking out for you. He did call in the strange vehicle," Asa said.

"No, Frank is nosy and likes to be in the middle of everything," Felicity corrected.

Hunter rubbed his jaw. "You had any other calls about this place?"

Asa shook his head. "Not that I'm aware of."

Hunter looked to Felicity who seemed to be understanding where his thoughts were headed.

"Well, I was just telling Hunter that I think someone has been here today. I left yesterday, and that bedroom door always stays closed. When we got here, it was open."

Asa's brow furrowed slightly. "You know of anyone else who has a key?"

Felicity shook her head. "No. Until recently, Cain Jenkins had a key. I assume either Dawn gave him one or he stole it. But I threw it in the bushes when he came by a few days ago."

Asa sucked air through his clenched teeth. "Do I need to know more about this? Cain is trouble."

Felicity twisted her finger. "Well, maybe. He was furious when he left." She swallowed hard. "He took Dawn's diamond earrings. And my dog."

Hunter's breath halted in his lungs. The guy stole her dog? What kind of a jerk did that?

"Did you file a police report?" Asa asked.

She shook her head. "No. I didn't know I could do that for the earrings since they were Dawn's, and I didn't know I could file one for my dog either."

"You can. We all know Cain at the station. He's a repeat offender. I don't know what we can do about either, but we can't do anything if we don't have your report. Do you have any documentation on the dog?"

Felicity straightened her posture. "Yes. He's a Black and Tan who answers to Boone. He's registered."

The excitement in Felicity's voice when she talked about her dog had Hunter's insides twisting. She'd lost her cousin, her dog, and apparently her home recently. Jameson's comment about her going through a tough time sounded like an understatement.

Asa jerked a thumb over his shoulder. "I'll be right back with a form."

"Thank you, thank you," Felicity said. She looked at Hunter, and her smile was brighter than he'd ever seen it.

Hunter took a deep breath. "If anyone can help get your dog back, it's Asa."

She covered her mouth, hiding her gorgeous smile. "I didn't even know I could file a police report. This just… This is great."

Asa returned with the document, and Felicity stepped aside to let him in. Hunter stayed standing as Asa explained the document to her. When she began writing, Asa left her at the table to give her some space.

Asa followed Hunter outside. The days were hit or miss for the coming spring weather or reminders of winter, but the nights were still frigid. Hunter needed a minute to wrap his head around the problems Felicity was facing.

"What are the chances of her getting the dog and earrings back?" Hunter asked.

"I can't make any promises. The dog may be easier than the earrings. If she has papers, I'm pretty sure we can get it back. She'll have to go to court about the charges, but that shouldn't be too complicated."

Hunter rubbed his brow. "Thanks. I'm glad you showed up."

"I wasn't interrupting anything?" Asa asked. His eyebrow rose on one side.

"No. Nothing like that. She just needed a ride tonight."

"She's been through a lot. Her mom was a wreck," Asa reminded Hunter.

He huffed. "Apparently, more than I realized."

"I'm just saying, be careful with her."

"What are you, her brother?" Hunter asked.

"You know what I mean. I know you're concerned about her, but why?"

"No reason."

"You're saying your interest in Felicity came out of nowhere? That doesn't happen."

"Yes, it can," Hunter argued.

"If you'd shut up for a second you'd realize I'm right and you should listen," Asa said.

Hunter rubbed the heels of his hands into his eyes. "I'm not in a relationship with her, so I don't need your dating advice."

The door opened, and Felicity handed the paper to Asa. "Thanks for this."

Asa inspected the document. "No problem. I'll keep you posted. You kids have a good night." He made a motion as if tipping his hat and slapped a hand on Hunter's shoulder. "See ya later, boss."

Asa's warning was laced with good intentions, and Hunter didn't want to consider the possibility that his friend had a point. Felicity had enough on her plate. She didn't need another complication. Not that he'd considered it an option, but erasing the thought of getting closer to Felicity from his mind was more difficult than he expected.

Felicity wrapped her arms around her middle and shivered. "I could use a cup of coffee. Too bad I already took my coffee maker to the ranch."

They stepped back inside, and the house seemed unnervingly quiet. A third person had been a safety buffer, but now he was alone with Felicity. After the events of the last few hours, he was looking at her in a different light, and it was only confusing his already mixed-up emotions.

Felicity yawned. "I'll just grab a few more things and we can get out of here."

"I'll take these to the truck," Hunter said as he picked up the bags she'd already filled in the kitchen.

He needed something to do and some space between himself and the woman in the next room.

Chapter Seven

FELICITY

The next morning, Felicity pushed herself out of bed in time for breakfast at the main house. If she was going to work around these people, she needed to get to know them. Hopefully, memorizing names would keep her mind off losing Dawn and Boone.

She stepped out into the early morning. The sun had barely risen, and Dixie was curled up on the porch. The dog perked her head up and stood.

"Hey, girl. I forgot that I don't have a ride." She reached down to scratch the dog's ears and looked for Jameson's truck. He'd said his place was a few cabins down, but she didn't know exactly which one. She should really pay him a visit soon. She at least owed him a cabin deep clean for getting her this job.

It didn't matter. His truck wasn't parked in front of any of the cabins lined beside hers. She reached into her pocket for her phone when she heard a door close. She looked up to see Hunter stepping out onto the porch of the cabin beside hers.

Did it mean anything that her heart rate jumped to a running speed when Hunter was around? She wanted to say it didn't, but it wasn't true. Hunter's kindness and patience yesterday had only heightened her curiosity. Everyone gave him a wide berth, but Felicity wanted to be sucked into that circle of loyalty he guarded so closely.

Hunter jerked his head toward the truck.

Felicity gave Dixie one last rub. "Looks like I found a ride."

She tucked her arms around her as she walked to the truck. Hunter was waiting with the passenger door open for her, and she climbed in.

He took his time walking around the truck and getting into the driver's seat. She wanted to say something—anything—but the words didn't come out.

When he parked in front of the main house, she worked up the courage to speak.

"Thanks for the ride."

"No problem. I can take you to pick your car up after supper. Beau said it should be ready."

"That would be great. You sure you don't mind?" Why couldn't she keep her mouth shut? She wanted to take him up on his offer, and she didn't want him to change his mind.

"I'm sure," he said resolutely.

He got out of the truck, and she assumed the matter had been settled. She followed him to the porch where he toed off his boots.

"You don't have to take yours off. Mama Harding just doesn't like the boots coming from the field into the meeting room."

"That makes sense." Felicity shivered thinking about the various nasty things those boots might spread around.

He opened the door and moved to the side for her to enter first. The big room where everyone ate meals was already full of cowboys and guests. She recognized a few faces, and she spotted Jameson nearby.

When he saw her, he waved and excused himself from the conversation he'd been having. "Morning. Ready to meet some more people?"

"I guess so. I actually need to find Haley. I'm starting work today."

Jameson lifted his chin and scanned the room. "There she is. Come on."

Felicity followed him toward a woman with auburn hair across the room. The one she assumed was Haley held a clipboard and pointed toward the front entrance as she spoke to a woman beside her.

Before they reached her, she made a note on her board and waved to the woman she'd been speaking to. When she caught sight of them, her eyes widened, and she gaped.

"Jameson, is this her?" she squealed.

"This is Felicity. Sis, this is Haley. She'll take good care of you."

"I sure will. I'm so glad you showed up. We'd been talking about adding an assistant manager around here, and the Lord provided." Haley opened her hand to indicate Felicity's serendipitous arrival.

"Assistant manager sounds important," Felicity pointed out.

"It is. You'll catch on quick, and we all kind of help each other out around here. You're never far from someone who can answer your question if I'm not around."

Felicity scanned the room, and her gaze landed on Hunter as if she were programmed to find him. He was watching her, but as soon as she spotted him, he turned his attention back to Noah who was talking to a group of the Harding brothers.

She knew most everyone's name from Jameson pointing people out across the room, but she spotted a few faces she couldn't put a name to. It was possible they were guests, but she didn't know how to tell them apart from the workers.

"After breakfast, we can start with a tour of the main house," Haley said, pointing around the room. "We'll work our way through the first floor and to the guest rooms upstairs."

"That would be great."

"Do you know everyone else?" Haley asked.

"Some of them."

Haley hooked an arm in Felicity's. "I'll introduce you. No offense, but Jameson is a typical guy. He's probably just left you to fend for yourself around here."

"I did not," Jameson countered. "I've just been busy."

"Oh, stop it," Haley waved. "I've got this. Go on and eat so you can get to work."

Jameson let his head fall back, and Felicity resisted the urge to giggle. She'd seen him do that hundreds of times when he was little. It was nice to know some things never changed.

"You can sit by me this morning, and I'll make sure you're in the know." Haley pointed to a bulletin board on the wall. "This is where we keep the notes about the ranch. Jade posts the children's activities schedule here, but most of it is for the guys."

"Looks like you've got a lot going on around here."

"Always, but you'll get used to it. The information board you and I will use is in the office. I'll show you that later. That's where you'll find check-in and checkout info, which rooms Laney has ready, and any repair issues that need to be addressed. Be sure to check it often because it's your job now to coordinate lining up repair workers if we need them. Then you make a note so we know when and where, since someone will have to be available when they arrive."

"Got it." Making sure things at the main house were in working order sounded like an important job, but the level of responsibility had Felicity feeling like she could be of service here.

A loud voice rose over the mutter of the crowd. It was Mama Harding standing at the end of the long counter where the food was displayed. "Okay, everyone. Line up. Guests first."

Felicity listened as Haley talked. They walked through the line, and Felicity ended up sitting between Haley and Levi, a talkative kid who told her everything she needed to know and didn't need to know about the ranch.

A few times during breakfast, Felicity glanced down the table to find Hunter watching her with those dark-green eyes. Before she'd eaten half her plate, she couldn't keep from glancing at him twice a minute. Oddly enough, he was usually looking back at her.

Focus. She needed something else to focus on. She asked Haley a question about the scheduling of guest activities and forced herself to stay turned toward Haley on her left instead of the cowboy to her right who was pushing his way into her every thought.

Hunter rose from his seat before anyone else and took his empty plate to the serving counter. Felicity watched as he snuck into a back hallway and didn't return.

Good. Now that he was gone, she might be able to learn how to do her new job.

After breakfast, Felicity followed Haley around, meeting a few people she hadn't been introduced to yet and getting a tour of the main house.

At lunch, Felicity tried not to notice Hunter's absence, but it gnawed at her like a dog on a bone. Her usual quietness was diminished to complete silence until Jameson shoved her shoulder.

"Hey, you okay?"

"Yeah. I'm just trying to remember half the things Haley told me today."

Jameson turned back to his plate. "You'll be fine. They give grace around here."

Felicity didn't want grace. She wanted to be helpful. Thankfully, it seemed as if there were always things that needed to be done around here.

She scanned the room for any other faces she knew that might be missing other than Hunter. Haley's husband was absent too. "Hey, where is Asher?"

"Oh, he went with Hunter to the auction. He'll be back by suppertime."

Why did knowing Hunter would be back soon send a thrill up her spine? She shouldn't care where he was or when he would return. The only person she'd kept tabs on lately was Dawn, and now it seemed as if she didn't have anything to look forward to at the end of the day. She hadn't kept up with her brother in years, and it seemed odd to start now.

Coming face-to-face with the personality trait that a former counselor had described as "a need to be needed" wasn't flattering. No one liked having someone hovering over them. Apparently, Dawn hadn't appreciated it either.

Maybe Felicity had been too pushy or too strict. Although her "no drugs in the house" rule seemed valid, Dawn had overdosed in her bedroom.

Should Felicity have been more aware or more lenient? She'd never know, and there wasn't a way to fix it now.

After lunch, Felicity followed Haley around the main house with her listening ears on. With her goal to focus on the new job, Felicity went the rest of the evening without thinking of Hunter.

Once they made their way around the house, Haley led Felicity back to the office where she explained everything from the pay scale to various weather contingencies. When they'd made their way through the online registration system and the various options and activities provided, Haley pushed her chair away from the computer.

"I think that's all the major things you'll need to know. Don't stress about learning everything right away. You can observe until you get the hang of things."

"Good because I feel like I've been drinking from a firehose all day."

Haley laughed. "Everything seems so simple to me now, but I've been here for the growth, so it was gradual to me."

"Have you always lived around here?" Felicity asked. She didn't recognize Haley, but that didn't mean they hadn't crossed paths in town before.

"No, I'm from Fort Collins, Colorado, but I'm sure glad I ended up here. I love this place."

"Me too. I feel like there's so much I haven't seen," Felicity said in wonder.

"There is *so* much. Asher and I sneak off on the ranch every time we get a chance." Haley's brow slightly furrowed. "You could come with us. Or maybe Jameson would take you."

Felicity laughed. "He's too busy. I don't want to bother him."

Haley tilted her head. "Asher told me a little about you and Jameson. He said you had it rough when you were young."

Felicity nodded. "That's right. Neither of us know our dads or if they were even two different people or the same man. Who knows? But our mom didn't make anything easy on us. So I took care of Jameson as much as I could." She huffed. "It's a wonder he made it this long."

Haley laid a hand on Felicity's arm. "You did a great job. Jameson is like part of the family around here. He's a great man. Don't sell yourself short." She lowered her chin. "I come from a big, loving family like this one. I have no idea how tough that must have been for the two of you."

Felicity straightened her shoulders. "I wouldn't wish it on anyone."

Haley stood, shaking the sadness from her expression. "Let's get back to work. We don't have long before supper, and I don't want to be gloomy when Asher gets back. He'll think I'm worried about the baby."

There wasn't even a bump that Felicity could distinguish, but she'd heard Haley was pregnant. "When are you due?"

"September. I'm hoping you'll be a pro at running this place by then so I can take a *long* maternity leave."

Felicity bit the inside of her cheek. "Take the time to appreciate the wonderful family you have."

Haley's grin was wide, and her eyes had a sheen. "You don't have to tell me twice." She clapped as if rallying attention for her next lesson. "Now, let's talk about the filing system. The Hardings are old school, so everything has a paper file as well as an electronic backup, thanks to me."

Hunter walked past the open office door, and Felicity tried not to stare. He probably got tired of people always gawking at him because of his scar, but that wasn't what drew her attention. It was something about the way he silently watched her, and excitement bubbled in her middle when she thought about riding with him to pick up her car later.

"Hunter!" Haley shouted.

He retraced his steps and stopped in the doorway.

"Can you help me get some boxes out of the storage closet? I want to show Felicity the filing system."

Hunter nodded and stepped to the side so Haley and Felicity could move out into the hallway.

"This way," Haley said as she pulled a key out of her pocket. "I'll get a key made for you, too, because you'll be filing when I'm out."

Felicity followed Haley through the laundry room of the main house where she unlocked a door on the far end. Hunter waited just behind Felicity, and she was hyper aware of his presence, despite his silence.

Once the door was unlocked, Haley stepped inside. "Okay, this is where we keep the old paper files. The newer ones are in the office."

The storage room was spacious and filled with boxes all clearly labeled. Plastic totes had the names of various holidays written on them, but the opposite wall was filled with shelves from floor to ceiling. The boxes on the shelves were labeled either accounting, health inspection, or releases.

"This is what you'll be filing," Haley said, pointing to the shelves. "Hunter, can you get one of each box, please?"

He grabbed the nearby step ladder and reached above his head for a box.

Now Felicity understood why they needed his help. Even on the step ladder, neither of them would have been able to reach the boxes on the top shelf.

Felicity's attention drifted lower and stalled when she saw the band of skin visible above his jeans. The reaching motion had lifted the hem of his T-shirt, revealing more scars. They covered almost every inch of his side that she could see.

She sucked in a startled breath and held it. Reacting to what she'd seen would embarrass them both.

Haley rested a hand on Felicity's arm and pinched her lips together as her eyes widened.

Hunter stepped off the step ladder and placed the box on an old desk before going back to get another.

She'd been doing a fairly good job of pushing thoughts of Hunter from her mind, but all progress was thrown out the window.

The scar that ran the length of one side of his face hadn't bothered her before. Now that she knew the deformity was worse than she'd realized, it felt like a wound on her own heart.

Sweat beaded on her neck, and her stomach rolled. How had he gotten those scars? It was hard to imagine what they'd been like when the wounds were fresh. How had he healed? An injury of that magnitude was life-changing.

When he'd retrieved the boxes, he looked to Haley as if awaiting further instruction.

"Thanks, so much. We'll just leave them here when we're finished, and I'll send Asher to put them back later."

Hunter nodded but didn't say anything. Felicity's breath halted as he stepped closer to her. It wasn't fear as much as a painful stab of recognition she felt when he was near. She wasn't a stranger to abuse, but Hunter's scars were different from anything she'd seen.

He paused beside her. "I asked Laney to pack us some sandwiches tonight so we can get on the road sooner. I can follow you to your old place after we get your car."

She did need to clean out the rental house. Stealing away the late hours every afternoon was making slow progress, but it was all she had until she got a day off. "Thanks. That would be great."

Without saying anything, he walked out of the room, leaving Felicity and Haley to do the work they came to do.

Haley opened the first box, but a somber expression clouded her usual upbeat features. "Hunter has dealt with and overcome a lot in his life, but he's a nice guy. You don't need to be scared of him."

"I'm not," Felicity hurried to clarify. "He's been good to me."

"Hunter is a good person, but there are some people in town who don't see it."

After Haley's defense of Hunter, she dove into the boxes. Neither of them mentioned him again as they worked, but Felicity wondered if he could be her key to getting back to good. If he could overcome a past of pain, couldn't she get over her grief of losing Dawn and Boone? Could Felicity forgive her mother for abusing and neglecting her for the first decade of her life?

Maybe she needed to take a page from Hunter's book—keep your head down, work hard, and do harm to no one.

It seemed like a good place to start.

Chapter Eight

HUNTER

Hunter was thankful for the sandwiches as he drove toward Beau's garage. With Felicity in the passenger seat beside him, he would have worried about the awkward silence if they weren't eating.

Felicity balled up the paper towel that had been wrapped around her sandwich as they pulled into the garage. "Thanks for handling supper."

Great. He'd treated a woman to a meal, and it was a grab-n-go sandwich. He was shattering all expectations around here. "You're welcome."

Felicity pointed out the window. "Is that Beau?"

Hunter saw his friend coming out of the office. He'd known Beau Lawrence most of his life, since the Lawrence farm was near Blackwater Ranch. Beau was a few years younger, but he had the kind of work ethic and loyalty Hunter appreciated in a man he often did business with. "Yeah. It's a little late for him to still be here."

They got out, and Hunter greeted his friend with a handshake.

"I was hoping you two would come by before I left." He extended a hand to Felicity. "I'm Beau."

She accepted the grease-stained hand without hesitating. "Felicity. Nice to meet you."

"I've known Jameson for a while, but I don't think we've crossed paths before."

Felicity shook her head. "I work a lot." She rolled her eyes and grinned. "And I think everyone in town knows Jameson."

Beau chuckled. "That's the truth. I wanted to talk to you about that tire." He pointed a thumb toward the building. "It's in my office if you have a minute."

"Sure," Felicity said. She looked at Hunter as if trying to silently ask what Beau might want to talk to her about.

Hunter shrugged and gestured for her to go first.

Inside Beau's office, every inch of every surface was covered in a gray film. Especially dark areas hung on the sides of the doors and frames in the shape of fingers, and a darker circle surrounded the doorknobs.

The tire sat propped against the wall, and Beau rolled it until he found the spot he was looking for. "This is your tire." He pointed to the three-inch gash on the road surface. "We don't see this often."

Felicity turned to Hunter, and she wore a fearful expression. "I was at the laundromat, and when I went to leave, I noticed it. I didn't want to assume it was slashed on purpose, but do you think it was?"

Hunter rubbed the stubble on his cheek. "I hate to say it, but it looks like it."

"That's what I thought too," Beau said. "I just wanted you to be aware."

"Thanks. I appreciate it. How much do I owe you?"

Beau handed her a paper from his desk. "Nothing. It's taken care of."

Felicity frowned at the receipt. "How?"

Hunter shook his head vigorously when Beau looked his way.

"I guess the ranch paid it," Beau offered.

Felicity snapped her head to Hunter. "I didn't tell them."

Hunter kept quiet. If he told her he'd paid it this morning, she'd insist on paying him back. If he didn't say anything, he wasn't actually lying to her.

She lowered the receipt and smiled at Beau. "Thank you. I'll be sure to thank the Hardings."

Hunter made a note to text his aunt when Felicity wasn't looking. Hard times sometimes meant broke times, and he didn't want Felicity worrying about something else when he had half a paycheck every month and nothing to spend it on.

Hunter followed Felicity to her old house and hoped the neighbor didn't call the police on him again. He had something to talk to her about, and he didn't want interruptions.

Inside, Felicity got straight to work. "I'll only be a minute," she promised.

Hunter followed her but stopped in the bedroom doorway. Resting his shoulder on the doorframe and crossing his arms over his chest, he asked, "Was it Cain?"

She didn't look up from the task. "I think so."

"That means he might be following you."

"Maybe. He could have just spotted my car in town."

Hunter didn't like either option. "Will you call Asa? He can add this to the police report."

She stopped working and tucked her chin. Her ponytail hung to her shoulder. "I will. I was just hoping he would go away."

"With a guy like Cain, I don't think that's likely."

She went back to work, and Hunter watched her as she efficiently packed the boxes and bags.

"Would you have told anyone if I hadn't been there?" Hunter asked.

"Maybe Jameson. I don't know."

"Why?"

She stopped what she was doing and looked up at him. "Because I don't need anyone. No one is going to look out for me except me." She laid a hand on her chest, emphasizing her independence.

"Jameson would," Hunter said.

"I'm the big sister. I've always taken care of him. I don't want him to worry about me."

Hunter could understand her need for independence. It was an attribute he admired, but he didn't want her to think she had to fight every battle alone. "You can tell me if you don't want to tell Jameson."

Her eyes softened, and Hunter wasn't sure if that meant he'd misunderstood or if she appreciated his offer.

"It's not weak to have help. I can't say I've ever done anything alone because I have my aunt, uncle, and cousins."

She tucked her chin again. "I guess that's true."

He moved to her side, and she didn't shy away from him. With one finger, he gently lifted her chin until those amber eyes were staring back at him.

"Word to the wise, keep your chin up. The weak go after the weak. Don't let them think you're like them."

Her mouth slowly morphed into a grin.

Emboldened by her smile, he continued, "Don't let your enemies see you struggling. Look them in the eye. Their mouth might lie, but their eyes tell the truth."

Her gaze flashed to his mouth and up to his eyes again. "Where'd you learn that?" she whispered.

"It was one of the lessons my dad taught me that actually made sense and didn't have anything to do with lying or getting away with murder."

She blinked up at him as if caught off guard. "What do you know about murder and lies?"

Those were the two important points she'd latched onto, and he couldn't blame her. He'd worked hard to forget everything his dad had taught him after he'd spent years separating every word into either the right or the wrong category.

Hunter let his finger fall, and her chin remained lifted. "Too much."

"I wish I were made of stone," she admitted. "It's exhausting acting like I'm fine all the time."

"Even stone isn't bulletproof. You've just got to know who to have in your corner."

She smiled up at him. There was a happiness there that he hadn't seen often since she came to the ranch, and he wanted more of this.

He wanted what he couldn't have.

"Like you?" she asked. "Are you someone I should have in my corner?"

Hunter nodded, and he couldn't tear his gaze from her. He needed to back away before he did something stupid, like kiss her.

He wanted to kiss her. He wanted to run his fingertips over her cheeks and thread his fingers into her hair.

"Was it your dad?" she asked.

And there was the knife that seemed to have a permanent home in his chest. He didn't like talking about his scars, but if it would help Felicity, telling her would be worth it.

"Only some of it."

"Where is he now?"

"I don't know."

"What about your mom?"

Hunter shook his head. He'd never had the slightest inkling who his mom was much less where she'd gone. "I never had any parents to speak of." It wasn't a sob story—just a fact. He'd had Silas and Anita, and they'd been like the parents he never deserved.

"Me either," she whispered.

Hunter didn't know anything about her dad, but he knew her mom didn't have a good reputation in Blackwater. He hoped Felicity hadn't been through half the things his dad had put him through.

"We're better off without them," he said.

Felicity bit her lips between her teeth. "I think you're right." She looked down and shuffled her feet. "I want to hope things are going to pick up from here."

"They will. The Hardings will be good to you." He wanted to tell her that he would be good to her too, but it wouldn't mean what she'd think. His M.O. was to do his helping from a distance.

Why was he standing so close to her? They'd been inching closer throughout the conversation, and he was close enough to notice the rise and fall of her shoulders with each breath.

He needed to put space between them, or he would give in to the temptation to kiss her. "Is there anything you need me to take to the truck? Any of the furniture?"

She took a step back and cleared her throat. "Um, that might be a good idea. I may donate some of this furniture, but I'd like to keep the table in the dining room and the coffee table in the living room. Jameson made them."

"I'll load those while you pack. I'll get the boxes when you're finished."

He'd planned on staying outside of her bedroom, but somehow he'd ended up well inside it. Before he made it to the hallway, she called out to him.

"Hunter?"

He turned and waited. Whatever she asked, he'd do it.

"I can't thank you enough for helping me with everything—the car and moving."

Hunter nodded. "Happy to help."

He wasn't sure if he'd ever been *happy* to help someone before, but with Felicity, it was true.

Chapter Nine

FELICITY

The first week on the ranch was immersive. Felicity followed Haley around and learned everything she could about the ranch and the bed and breakfast.

The only area she'd shied away from was the stables. Lucas and Maddie made hanging out with the horses sound like fun, but Felicity knew better. Horses were powerful and unpredictable. After the crazy month she'd had, she needed to stay in her lane.

Except when it came to Hunter. She kept her curiosity subtle, but after his assurances the last time he'd helped her at the rental house, all ability to push thoughts of him from her mind was thrown out the window.

She'd never felt so understood. Hunter had a way of recognizing her fears and sadness and making it seem as though she were capable of bravely overcoming anything.

The counselors hadn't been able to give her that courage. How could Hunter embolden her with so few words?

There truly were *few* words. Hunter hadn't muttered so much as a one-word greeting in her direction in over a week. Granted, she'd spent little time around him. She saw him at every meal, but he was often the last to arrive and the first to leave, always rushing off to manage some task on the ranch.

It should've been fine. She didn't *need* to talk to him, except she wanted to. She had no idea what they would talk about, but she ached to hear more of his deep words full of assurance and encouragement. He'd overcome so much, and she wanted a piece of whatever kept his chin up, as he'd advised her to do.

Jameson also wasn't around as much as she'd expected. Between the ranch and the fire station, his plate was overflowing, and she gave him a wide berth when he was busy.

They'd both been able to take the same day off this week, and they'd finished cleaning out the rental house. After deciding that it was better to rip the bandage off than sit around and mope over

Dawn's things, she boxed it all up and donated everything to Blackwater Restoration. Felicity had never needed any of her cousin's things before, and she doubted she'd need anything in the future.

The only thing she needed to do was meet with her landlord and terminate the lease. There was a hefty fine, but it was less than paying out the remaining months in rent on her own.

Getting rid of the things that reminded her of Dawn should have given her some kind of closure. Why did she still want to call her cousin to check in? Why did her cabin feel so quiet? Keeping Dawn out of trouble had been a full-time job, and she was having a hard time shifting gears.

Felicity hadn't seen Haley since lunch when they'd parted ways. Felicity guided the guests to their various activities on the ranch, while Haley had manned the phones and responded to emails. It was thirty minutes until suppertime when they met back up in the office.

"Oh, I got distracted and forgot to call you," Haley said, slapping her hand to her forehead. "We're having a meal planning party. Can you come?"

A meal planning party? Felicity hadn't been in charge of the meals here or anywhere else before, and she didn't know what this *party* entailed. "What is that?"

"Well, this will be our first time, but we're making freezer meals. We like to have plenty of soups and casseroles on hand so Mama Harding can take a day off every now and then. Plus, Camille and I want to stock up at our own places a little before the babies come, so this is a trial run."

"I've never done anything like that before. I wouldn't be much help."

Haley laughed. "Did you hear me say that we haven't done this before either? We all just kind of want a reason to sneak away together for a few hours. Girl time is always appreciated around here where we're often outnumbered by the men."

Felicity chuckled. "I'm used to being outnumbered. I came from the lumber mill, remember?"

"Oh." Haley made a sour face. "That sounds awful. You need some girl time too."

"When?"

"Tonight."

"After supper?" Felicity asked.

"No, Mama Harding and Maddie are sticking around for supper. Mama made us sandwiches to munch on while we work, and she handed over some of her special recipes." Haley clapped and bounced in her seat.

Felicity was slowly getting used to Haley's unwavering peppy personality, and she kind of wished she had half a fraction of that excitement about anything.

Despite the nagging feeling that she might not completely fit in with the Harding women, Felicity agreed. "Okay."

"We're going over to Camille's house. You can ride with me. Let's go get the sandwiches. I think Camille and Jade bought the stuff we need today."

Felicity followed Haley into the meeting room. She stopped to say hello to everyone, and Felicity tried to offer her own greeting hoping that some of her boss's friendliness would rub off on her.

In the kitchen, Mama Harding pointed to a bag on the counter. "Those are yours. Have fun tonight."

"We will, Mama." Haley kissed her mother-in-law on the cheek before grabbing up the bag.

Felicity followed again as Haley made her way back into the meeting room. The men and guests were starting to fill the room. Every evening seemed like an event at the main house.

Jameson spotted them as they made their way toward the door and quirked his brow. "Where are you headed?"

Felicity noticed Hunter standing behind her brother. His expression was harder than usual, and she wanted to erase the lines between his brows and bring back the soft expressions she'd seen from across the room throughout the past week.

"We're making freezer meals," Felicity said.

Jameson held up his hands. "Unless it involves a grill, I'll let you have that one."

Haley laughed. "I wouldn't trust you to make jerky. I remember that taco pie you tried to pass off as edible last year."

"The oven in my cabin is junk!" Jameson defended.

"It's a good thing you have Mama Harding," Felicity pointed out. She said the words casually, but it was clear that Mama Harding and the rest of this family were incredible blessings in her brother's life.

Now, she got to experience a little of their kindness, and it felt like a game changer. She was getting a chance to get on her feet after a series of tragedies, and she wasn't sure how she'd made it this far without their encouragement.

Jameson pointed toward the kitchen. "Speaking of Mama, I think I'll go see if she needs a hand."

"Don't burn anything!" Haley yelled at his back. "Come on, they're waiting for us." She grabbed Felicity's hand, dragging her toward the door.

She gave Hunter one last look, and the tension in his stance eased a fraction as his frown fell away.

"This way," Haley prodded.

"Right." Freezer meals were the focus for tonight, but why couldn't she think of anything except Hunter's captivating green eyes?

***

There hadn't been a lull in the conversation all evening, and Felicity felt her shoulders relaxing with each passing minute. She listened and followed instructions for the meal prep while the women talked.

She'd made fast friends with most of the women at the ranch, but hearing their casual conversations made them seem more down-to-earth and less like the well-put-together women she'd envisioned.

Jade sprinkled seasonings over the casserole dishes. "I love it that he is so independently driven, but can't he wait until the sun rises?" Apparently, her five-year-old soon-to-be stepson, Levi, thought the workday began at five in the morning.

Haley laughed. "At least that means an early bedtime. I don't know how that kid goes ninety-to-nothing all day long."

"Amen," Jade added. "I'm tired. And with the wedding coming up, I have my hands full." Jade and Aaron had decided on a small wedding. A very small wedding with only the officiant and their parents at the church.

"We're all here to help," Laney reminded her.

Haley perked up. "Everything for the wedding is taken care of. Relax."

Jade rested her head on Haley's shoulder. "I'm so glad you're my tiny wedding planner. You're a rock star."

"That's what I'm told," Haley said. "These are ready."

Camille laid a hand on Jade's shoulder. "I forgot to tell you, Sheila Darty came in the thrift store the other day and said her daughter was considering homeschooling little Amy. I told her I'd give you her number so you two could talk about it."

"Yes! I'd be happy to," Jade said.

"Of course. You talk about curriculums like some people talk about their favorite TV shows," Haley joked.

Jade lifted a finger. "It's actually curricula."

Haley laughed. "You know everything."

Jade lowered her chin but continued mixing the meatloaf with her hands. "Everything except how to be a mom."

"You're kidding, right? You're already a mom," Camille said.

"No, I've been a nanny and a teacher, but being a mom is different," Jade said.

Camille leaned against the counter beside Jade. "You've never been just a nanny or a teacher to Levi. You know that, right?"

"I just want to be good for him. He deserves a good mom."

"And that's you," Haley pointed out. "You're getting cold feet when you've been doing a great job all along."

"Group hug!" Camille shouted.

Felicity chuckled. Of course, Camille would think hugs solved the world's problems. But as they all gathered to embrace Jade who held her meat mixture covered hands out so she didn't get it on her friends, Felicity wondered if the love and support of a group like this could really solve life's problems.

"Enough of this negativity. Jade, you're gonna be the best mom," Camille stated, then she turned to Felicity. "How are you liking things here?"

"I love it," Felicity said, nodding emphatically. "I'm glad I get to be close to Jameson again."

"What was it like growing up with him? He's always such a gentleman," Haley said.

Felicity's smile quirked. "He wasn't always a gentleman. When he was about six, I didn't think either of us were going to make it. He was into everything."

"I bet your parents had a time with him," Jade said.

Felicity's smile fell, and the room grew quiet. Everyone looked at her, unsure what to say.

Jade looked around. "What?"

"Um, my parents weren't around a lot," Felicity said.

"Oh," Jade drawled. "I'm sorry. I didn't know."

"It's fine." Felicity waved a hand. "I don't know much about our dads at all, but Mom was more interested in her next fix than fixing dinner."

Jade stopped mashing in the meatloaf. "That's terrible. Jameson is always so happy. I had no idea."

Felicity shrugged. "We always had each other. I made sure he had food, and when Mom died, it wasn't much of a surprise. She'd been killing herself for years with anything and everything she could get her hands on."

"Oh no," Haley said, raising a hand to cover her quivering chin. "And then Dawn…"

Felicity nodded. "Yeah. We were close in age, and we grew up together. Her mom tried to help when our mom would go off on a bender, so she felt a lot like my sister instead of my cousin."

Felicity's throat felt tight, and a familiar tingling began in her nose. She tried to swallow the emotion crawling up her throat, but it was no use. Her hands began to shake, and she tucked them around her middle.

"We're so sorry," Camille said as she wrapped Felicity in a tight embrace.

Burying her face in her friend's shoulder, she let the dam holding the flood of tears break. Clinging to Camille, she cried again for Dawn. "I miss her so much," she mumbled.

More hands rubbed her back. "We can't replace Dawn, and we don't want to, but you have us now," Laney whispered.

Felicity's shoulders shook as her well ran dry. She'd been holding it in for so long, it was a relief to let it out.

After the rush of emotions, she raised her head and wiped her cheeks. "I'm sorry."

"Nothing to be sorry for. You're in a room full of women," Haley said, holding her arms out to encompass the group.

Felicity chuckled and wiped at her face again. "I'm not used to this."

Haley shook her head. "Yeah, I can't imagine growing up without my mom and sisters. They've always been my rock."

"Same," Jade said. "But now I'm blessed with more family, and I love them just as much."

Felicity rolled her eyes. "Jameson was always a boy through and through. No crying around him."

"Oh, I bet he's a total softie for you," Haley said.

"He's…" Felicity paused, unwilling to let the tears begin again. "He's the best. He's always been my rock and my reason to keep going. It wasn't always easy, but it was easier when I thought about him and how he didn't deserve the way our mom neglected him."

"He sure speaks highly of you," Laney said.

"He does?"

Laney nodded. "I overheard him asking Silas and Anita if they had a job for you. Of course, they said yes right away, but he added in a few good words about you before he ran out the door."

"I'm glad they took a chance on me. I lost my job when Dawn died."

Camille laid a hand on Felicity's shoulder. "I'd like to pray for you."

"Okay. I mean, thank you."

Camille closed her eyes and bowed her head. "Father…"

Felicity hadn't expected a prayer right this minute. People often said the familiar, "Praying for you," but she wondered if that statement would hold more truth if people stopped what they were doing and prayed in the moment it was on their hearts.

She held Camille's hand on one side and Laney's on the other. Surrounded by friends, she felt accepted and understood.

When Camille uttered "Amen," they all raised their heads and wiped their eyes.

Haley walked to the other side of the kitchen. "Ugh. Hormones are fierce."

Everyone chuckled, but Camille kept an assuring hold on Felicity's hand. "Will you come to church with us tomorrow?"

Felicity bit the inside of her cheek. The last few weeks had been full of moving to the ranch and getting things tied up at her old place, and she felt a weight of longing for the community of a church family. "Okay. I'd like that."

"Do you already have a church?" Jade asked.

"I do. I love it there, but I'd really like to visit yours." Trusting in the strength of their faith, she felt confident the message would be at least somewhat enlightening. The Harding family had faith coming out of the woodwork around this place.

"Jameson comes with us," Laney added.

"You all go together?" Felicity asked.

Jade nodded. "Yep. Sometimes, we're missing Noah, Lucas, and Jameson when they're on shift at the fire station, but everyone else goes. Getting this many people to church on time after they get up for morning chores takes dedication." She smiled at the group of ladies. "I think we'll be half the church congregation soon."

"One person at a time," Camille said. "Our family sure has grown in the last few years."

"Hunter goes too?" Felicity asked.

Haley tried to stifle a grin by biting her lips between her teeth.

"Even Hunter," Camille confirmed. "Every Sunday."

"I know what you're thinking," Laney said. "Hunter might be rough around the edges, but don't judge that book by its cover. He's scarred, but he has a great heart."

Haley had picked up another sandwich and covered her mouth to hide her chewing. "He's a big ol' teddy bear."

"He would hide in his cabin for weeks if he heard either of you saying nice things about him,"

Jade said. She leaned over to whisper to Felicity. "He hates attention."

"He sure gets a lot of it for someone who doesn't want to be seen," Felicity pointed out.

"Oh, he's seen," Camille said. "Some people gawk and stare at the scars, but other people see the good that he does around here, and that's all that matters. He does the landscaping at church and refuses payment. He helps at the Lawrence farm when they need extra hands. He takes Dixie to the vet when she needs to go. If people looked at more than his face, they might see who he really is."

Felicity rubbed the side of her cheek and yawned. "Why does he have the scars?"

Laney grinned. "I've never heard it from Hunter himself, and I imagine he wouldn't tell it like the others do, but it's really something to hear."

They all nodded, and now Felicity's casual curiosity had grown into something unquenchable. She remembered when Hunter had disappeared from school, and she recalled later seeing him in town looking like a different person. He couldn't have been more than sixteen. "What do you mean?"

"He saved Lucas's life," Jade said.

Felicity couldn't stifle her gasp. Hunter had taken on a life-long burden of physical change to help someone else.

Camille rested a hand on Felicity's shoulder. "It's okay. Everyone survived, and that's what matters most. I don't think anyone in this family who knows what really happened could ever forget what he did."

Laney rested her arms on the counter. "Lucas was about ten years old when he was trapped by a pack of wild dogs. Hunter distracted them so Lucas could get away, and they attacked. He fought them off, but he barely made it. Micah said the doctors estimated he had about fifty bites and hundreds of stitches. I think there were three surgeries."

Camille nodded. "Yeah, and his dad had only been gone for about a year, so Mama Harding made sure he went to all his appointments and helped him through therapy. He had to drop out of school, but she made sure he got his GED."

"Yay for education," Jade shouted, breaking the heavy tone of the conversation.

Laney continued, "With his dad's scandal still fresh in the news around here, Hunter disappearing for a while made everyone suspect he was teaming up with his dad or something. So that bad rap got stuck to him when he didn't deserve it."

"What did his dad do?" Felicity asked.

Camille shrugged. "I guess it won't hurt to tell you. Almost everyone around here knew some variation of the story back then. He stole from the ranch and ran off. I don't know how much, but Noah said it was enough that they almost lost the whole place."

"And he did that to his family?" Felicity asked.

"Butch was always out for himself. Silas might be his brother, but they were night and day. And Silas never wanted to give up on Butch."

Having a sibling of her own, Felicity wondered if she would do the same. Dawn had tested Felicity's trust more than once, but she'd never given up on trying to help her cousin.

Considering Butch probably didn't have anyone else he could turn to, it was easy to believe Silas would be reluctant to abandon his brother.

"That same fierce loyalty is in all the Hardings. They're not quitters," Camille said. "So, Hunter never did anything wrong, but living with his dad's betrayal, the physical disfigurement, and being abandoned will change a person."

Change a person? Felicity was certain those things would have crippled her, leaving her either a broken shell or full of anger at the injustice. It was a wonder Hunter could keep his chin up and face the hatred of the world every day.

Haley yawned. "We all appreciate Hunter, and we're glad to have you and Jameson here too now."

Felicity rubbed her eyes. "Me too."

"I'm about to turn into a pumpkin. Sorry to cut out early, but baby and mama need sleep," Haley said as she stretched her arms above her head. "Night, ladies."

"I'll finish the meatloaf," Laney said. "Y'all can go."

"I'll help," Felicity offered. She needed something to keep her mind busy, or she'd be up all night thinking of the man in the cabin beside hers who risked everything to save his family.

Chapter Ten

HUNTER

It was full dark, and the cloudless sky dotted with stars seemed to reach on forever.

Hunter liked the quiet nights. When the cattle were in the pastures closer to the cabins, he heard everything. When a calf was being born, the mother wailed into the night, and Hunter usually put his boots on and went to make sure everything went well.

The mountain lions made a sound that would make the hair on the back of his neck stand up, and foxes sounded like a woman screaming.

When the night was quiet, he usually slept best. He'd have no such luck tonight because he knew Felicity wasn't home from Camille's house yet, and he wouldn't close his eyes until the cabin door closed behind her.

The ranch wasn't inherently dangerous, except when it was. No one had a way to predict when the wild animals would venture close to the cabins, and he didn't want to take that chance with Felicity out here alone at night.

He strummed a familiar tune on the guitar, and Dixie's head perked up. The dog had some special sense that knew Felicity was coming before her headlights crested the hill from Noah and Camille's place.

Dixie got to her feet and stood at attention beside him, patiently waiting for Felicity to come home.

Hunter was like a dog—loyal despite rational reasons to leave well enough alone.

Felicity parked in front of her cabin and got out slowly. He could barely make out her silhouette in the dark, but her shoulders seemed heavy with exhaustion.

She stretched her neck as she approached the porch, and Hunter swallowed hard. She wore her hair up often, which meant he was eternally tempted by the smooth skin of her neck. What he wouldn't give to trail his lips over it and kiss the thrumming of her pulse that called to him every time he looked her way.

If it wasn't her skin and lips tempting him, it was her eyes. It was all in his head, but he imagined those subtle, shy looks she gave him were silently begging him to come closer. He'd been transfixed a few times, and he'd almost let that undiluted desire get the best of him.

But he was the only one between the two of them who wanted that. Assigning silent words to Felicity's looks was one thing, but she hadn't actually said anything that would lead him to believe she wanted that kind of attention from him.

Who would? He could win a casting call for the villain in any fairy tale retelling.

His fingers brushed over the strings of the guitar. Felicity was home, and his self-imposed mission was complete.

As the low vibrations filled the air, Felicity's footsteps on the porch halted.

Great. He'd scared her and drawn attention to himself. Neither of those things was intended.

"Hunter?" she whispered into the night.

"Yeah."

"Are you playing?"

"I was."

She changed her course and walked back off the porch. She was headed for his cabin, and he had no idea what he'd just done.

Dixie met her between the cabins and walked with her to his porch. Felicity sat on the top step and leaned her back against the wooden column. Dixie promptly laid beside her, head resting in Felicity's lap.

"Can you play one for me?" she asked.

He hesitated. He played for a room full of people at Barn Sour at least one weekend a month, but this was a different audience.

"Just one, please."

Focusing on the song would keep his mind off the captivating woman sitting inches from the toe of his boot, so he chose a song and played. That was one thing he loved most about music—it was freeing. It required his focus, and he couldn't think about anything else while the music needed his attention.

When the last chord vibrated in the guitar against his chest, he waited to see if she would really only stay for one song.

"Will you sing?" she asked.

He shook his head, then thought better of it since she couldn't see him in the dark. "I don't sing."

"Why not?" she questioned.

He thought about the truth and decided telling her anything else would be a lie. "My dad told me to shut up, so I did."

She was looking up at him, but he couldn't see her expression. "What a waste of happiness."

"I don't think hearing me sing ever brought anyone happiness," he said matter of factly.

"How do you know? Have you done it?"

"Not in about twenty years." Well, no one had *heard* him sing in the last two decades. He sang quietly in his cabin sometimes when he couldn't sleep.

"Why would you listen to him but not to me?"

A twinge of hurt clouded her question, and Hunter didn't want to answer.

Instead, he lifted one side of his shirt, exposing the jagged scars that covered his torso. She wouldn't be able to see them clearly in the dark, and it fueled his courage.

"Because some of these are from wild dogs, but some are from him." He lowered the shirt. "Words don't hurt, but they feel like they do when your skin is burning."

There. That would put an end to her questions. It would also seal his fate and forfeit any chance he might have had of making something real out of this fascination he had with Felicity Ford.

"I know." She shifted to turn her shoulders away from him and pulled up the sleeve of her shirt. "You can't see it, but it's a burn. I was nine."

Hunter didn't say anything. He didn't move while time seemed to stand still.

"Jameson was a baby, and Mom was handing him over to me so she could go to sleep. I was expected to get up in the night if he woke. When she laid him in my arms, her cigarette hit my arm, but I couldn't jerk away or I'd drop him."

She put her sleeve back down and sighed. "I'm just glad it wasn't him. He cried constantly anyway, and a burn like that would have kept him up all night until it healed."

He knew what a cigarette burn felt like. It was like pain and numbness mixed into a searing, unrelenting agony.

"I saw your scars. Earlier when we were in the storage closet," she whispered. "One stuck out to me, and I knew it was a burn and not like the others."

His chest ached, and it was difficult to breathe. He didn't care so much that she saw his scars, but seeing hers and hearing about her mom caused almost a physical pain inside him.

Anger and anguish roiled in his middle. Felicity never deserved to be hurt.

"You heard anything about your dog?" he asked, needing to change the subject before his blood pressure reached stroke levels.

She rested her head back against the column. "Nothing yet. Asa said he would call me. I don't need to bother him while he's doing his job."

Asa would call her as soon as he had any news. Hunter was sure of it.

"You need any more help at the house?" he asked.

"No. Jameson helped out, and I think we got everything. I called my aunt about Dawn's stuff, but she didn't want it. She said it would be too hard to go through."

He couldn't imagine what a parent would feel after losing their kid. Funny enough, his own parents hadn't seemed to care at all.

He scratched his chin and readjusted the guitar in his lap. "You heard anything else about Cain?"

She shook her head. "No, but I'm guessing that's a good thing. I just hope he didn't hurt Boone."

"Cain will have another run-in with the law soon, and they'll probably have a chance to get your dog back."

She chuckled once. "Is it terrible if I hope that happens? I shouldn't wish for someone to break the law, but I really miss Boone."

She didn't have to say it. He knew she loved that dog. Cain had stolen Felicity's happiness, and that put him on Hunter's black list.

"If he gives you any trouble, you can call me." The thought of her being in danger felt a lot like someone was filleting his insides.

"Okay."

Apparently, caring about Felicity caused his rational thoughts to cease while instinct reined because he couldn't get her out of his head.

Not that it mattered. She was too good for him, and no one deserved an ugly shell of a man. It wouldn't do him any good to want what he couldn't have.

She stood, rousing Dixie from her rest. "I should get home."

Home. Her home was right beside him, and the thought pleased him more than it should.

Despite her declaration, she hesitated. "Good night."

"Good night." He didn't stand, knowing he wouldn't be going inside until she was safely home.

Dixie followed her to the cabin next door, and Hunter released a tired breath when she closed the door. The early morning was going to be brutal.

He fell into bed and stared at the shadows the moonlight cast throughout the room. Sleep wouldn't come until he checked in with Asa. Hunter knew his friend was already off work, so he typed out a quick text.

Hunter: Any word on Felicity's dog?

The reply was quick.

Asa: Nothing yet, but I'm keeping an eye on Cain.

That was enough to settle the unease Hunter was feeling, but another text dinged just after the first.

Asa: I'm looking out for her. And praying.

Hunter: Thanks.

He didn't always turn to prayer first, but maybe that was what he needed to do right now. Outside of keeping his eyes open to any danger from Cain, Hunter felt a dread that he recognized as helplessness.

If he couldn't do anything else, praying was the least he could do.

Chapter Eleven

FELICITY

Her first month on the ranch had been transformative. She'd eaten better, slept well, and had been happier than ever. If she'd known the ranch was in the healing business, she'd have signed up years ago.

Swapping glances with Hunter all month also made her feel like a teenager with a crush, so she was lamenting the loss of that youth right about now. Her life had gone by so fast.

Not that Hunter seemed to lack energy. He was up before the sun every morning and worked until after dark without complaint.

Felicity brushed through her hair and studied her reflection in the mirror. It had been a long time since she'd had a haircut, put on makeup, or even thought about applying moisturizer, and the effects were harrowing. When had she lost that youthful look? Somewhere between twenty-five and thirty, it seemed. A stranger was looking back at her. How much had that loss of her self-care cost her?

Any chance of finding a man to love her like this seemed gone now. But, if he didn't love her despite her looks, did he even love her at all?

She'd probably never know the answer to that one, and the realization pricked her heart. She cared so deeply about the people she loved, but the kind of love shared between a husband and wife seemed lost to her.

A knock at the door startled her, and she turned from the mirror. Her fear was silly. It was someone from the ranch, and none of them meant her harm.

She did wish the old wooden door had a peephole. Old habits died hard.

Opening the door slowly, she was surprised to see Hunter standing on the porch looking tired. Her own exhaustion was probably evident as well.

"Hey. Is everything okay?" she asked. He'd never paid her a visit, except for the times he brought her meals when she'd first arrived.

"Yeah, I just…"

He was either nervous or confused, but either worried her.

"Hunter?" she asked, wishing he'd quit stalling and tell her what was the matter.

"Nothing is wrong. I didn't sleep much." He rubbed his face as if trying to wake himself. "I just wanted to make sure you're okay."

"Yes. Why wouldn't I be?"

Hunter shook his head. "I'm still half asleep. I just needed to lay eyes on you this morning, okay?"

She tried to swallow the lump that had formed in her throat, but she couldn't. He was worried about her? Worrying over other people was *her* job. "I'm okay," she whispered, then cleared her throat. "You don't have to lose sleep over me. I can take care of myself, but thank you."

Hunter hung his head. "Sorry. I can't help it."

She rested a hand on his arm, and his attention lifted to her.

"I've never needed anyone before. Really, I'm okay." He didn't make her feel weak, and that made all the difference. Instead, the comfort of his presence made her feel as if it was finally okay to break.

Hunter narrowed his eyes as if waiting for her to say more. "You sure about that?"

Her brow wrinkled as she tried to think about what he might be referring to. She had accepted his help getting things from her old place, but it wasn't a need so much as a want.

But there was one time, several years ago, when she'd truly needed help. She'd prayed, and help had come, but she had no idea about who had saved her or how she'd made it out alive. The memory of Dawn's ex-boyfriend's fist connecting with her face stung as if the pain were real again. Over and over, he'd broken the bones of her face while his new girlfriend kicked at her side. It was a miracle only two ribs had been broken.

Felicity had been praying for relief—either by death or a savior—when she'd lost consciousness. She'd woken in the hospital, attended by a kind nurse who assured Jameson that the injuries would heal in time.

She'd assumed Jameson had found her, but he claimed he'd gotten the call from the hospital.

Her breaths were shallow as she wondered about that night and the painful weeks after when her mother had stolen her pain medication.

Hunter took a step back. "I shouldn't have come."

"Wait!" She reached for him, hoping that her hesitation hadn't made him think she was ungrateful for his thoughtfulness.

He was moving too fast, and she didn't have shoes on yet. He was off the porch and she was running after him, dodging Dixie, when she saw Jameson.

Hunter realized at the same moment that they had an audience, and from the look on Jameson's face, he wasn't happy.

"What's going on? What did you do to her?" The crease between his brows grew deeper as his attention flickered between them. "Did you stay with her?"

The accusation in his voice and his words was like a slap in the face. It stole her breath for a moment. Sure, Hunter had been spotted leaving her cabin early in the morning when she still didn't have shoes on, and while that might be the first thing that came to mind, her brother had certainly made a quick assumption.

"Are you serious?" Hunter seethed.

His tone wasn't helping the situation at all. In fact, it stoked the flames of Jameson's anger.

"Him?" Jameson asked. "Really?"

"Jameson," Felicity reprimanded.

Hunter's shoulders swelled, but he didn't retaliate. She could have kissed him in that moment for the willpower it must have taken to let that jab slide off him.

Jameson turned back to Hunter. "She's my sister."

Hunter pointed at her but kept his attention on Jameson. "She's a grown woman. Why don't you treat her like one?"

Felicity only had time to gasp as Jameson's fist launched toward Hunter. Every muscle in her body tensed as she prepared for the impact.

But it never came. The underwhelming slap she heard was that of Jameson's knuckles colliding with Hunter's hand.

He'd caught the punch and stopped it.

She couldn't breathe. The look on Jameson's face was a mask of confusion. Her brother wasn't a small man for his early twenties, but Hunter was broad and hardened by years of physical labor.

It would take a lot of strength to stop that punch, and silence fell around the three of them as realization set in.

A door slammed, and they all looked to see who was joining the altercation.

Little Levi barreled off the porch of his cabin down the line. "Uncle Hunter! Jameson! What are you doing?"

The boy's innocent question broke the tension between the two men, and they lowered their arms. Aaron followed his son with a hard look on his face, no doubt wondering what exactly had been going on before Levi's interruption.

Jameson turned to Levi, and Felicity saw the look on her brother's face—shame.

"We were working on a new handshake," Jameson said.

Please let him believe it. Please let him believe it. Jameson was being a blockhead, but she didn't want Aaron upset with her, her brother, or Hunter for fighting in front of his son.

"Can you teach me?" Levi asked excitedly.

"Sure," Jameson said. "After breakfast."

"I can eat more than you," Levi taunted.

"You probably can today. I've lost my appetite," Jameson said.

Aaron nudged Levi's shoulder. "Go on to the truck. I'm right behind you."

Aaron waited until Levi was out of earshot to ask, "What was that?"

Hunter didn't move or speak. Jameson's glance cut to Hunter as if waiting for him to explain.

"It's nothing," Felicity said. "Just a misunderstanding."

Aaron narrowed his eyes at the two other men. "Quit fighting and make up a handshake before breakfast."

"Got it," Jameson responded, seeming to have lost his rage from only moments ago.

No one spoke until Aaron left them. When the truck started up, Felicity stepped up beside her brother.

"Have you lost your mind?"

Jameson stared back at her as if the question might be a trap. He was young, but he was too old to be flying off the rails like that.

She pointed at Hunter. "He was checking on me. Innocently, might I add. Where do you get off thinking he would hurt me, or better yet, sleep over?" Her volume was rising along with the pitch of her voice. She'd be calling dogs or breaking glass if she kept on this trajectory.

She crossed her arms over her chest and willed her voice to deepen. "Hunter has been good to me, and you are way out of line."

Jameson rubbed the back of his head. "I know. I got carried away. I mean, I assumed the worst because you looked upset, and I didn't really expect him to be here." He took a deep breath and faced Hunter. "I wouldn't have expected you to check on her, but thanks."

Hunter nodded but didn't say anything.

"Now, can we play nice and go to breakfast?" she asked.

Jameson pointed at her bare feet. "As soon as you get some shoes on."

"Right. I'll be there in a minute." She'd lost all feeling in her toes.

Jameson started toward his truck, but Hunter didn't leave.

When Jameson was gone, she stepped closer to Hunter. "Thanks for not knocking him out."

Hunter's mouth pulled up on one side in an adorable half smile. The scar didn't run through his lip, but she guessed that the muscles in his face could have been impacted from the injury, creating a grin that she appreciated all the more for its rarity and uniqueness.

"You'd probably never speak to me again if I leveled your brother."

She shrugged. "He deserved it, but I'm glad it didn't come to that."

Hunter nodded slowly. His gaze was locked with hers, and she couldn't turn away.

"Can I give you a ride to breakfast?" he asked.

The hope in her heart grew wings and soared. "I'd like that."

Hunter tentatively reached for her hand and locked his fingers with hers. Her palm tingled where their skin touched, and she tightened her grip. When had touching hands with a man ever been so impactful?

Never. Because there wasn't anyone in the world like Hunter Harding.

"I'll wait for you by the truck," he said, giving her hand a gentle squeeze before releasing it.

With that small touch, a gate had been opened within her, releasing every bit of tension she'd been carrying. It flooded from her body, allowing her to breathe again.

"I'll be quick."

She jogged back to her cabin and pulled on her boots. Leaving her hair down for right now, she grabbed the hair tie to pull it up on the way.

Hunter waited by the passenger side of his truck and opened the door when she approached. She climbed into the large diesel truck with a soft "Thank you."

Neither of them spoke on the way to the main house, and she took the time to pull her hair up. From the corner of her eye, she could see Hunter watching her, dividing his attention between her and the trail ahead.

"What?" she asked.

Hunter stopped looking at her and focused on driving. "I like your hair up."

"Really? I would think it's prettier down."

"It's beautiful both ways, but I can see more of your face when it's up."

Heat rushed to her cheeks. "Thank you." She'd been thinking she needed to do something different with her hair just this morning, but if Hunter liked it, she wouldn't dare change it.

"Thanks for the ride," she said as he parked in front of the main house.

He didn't say anything as he got out and met her in front of the truck. Hunter didn't need to say every little thing that was expected. The things he did say were important, and she cherished every word he chose to give her.

They were a little late for breakfast, so they fell into line together. Jameson was just sitting down at the largest table, and it looked as if Silas had already blessed the food.

She filled her plate at the buffet-style counter and chose a seat at the farthest end of the long table. Some people were already beginning to stand with their empty plates. She held her breath as Hunter sat in the chair beside her.

The only way to hide her smile was to eat, so neither of them said anything as they hurried to catch up with the others who'd gotten a head start on the meal. Jameson glanced their way a few times, but she made no expressions to reveal what she was thinking.

When Hunter had finished eating, he looked her way and said, "Are you off today?"

"Yeah."

"Would you like to come out on the ranch with me?" he asked with a hint of nervousness in his tone. "You don't have to if you don't want—"

"I do," she interrupted. "I have some errands to run this morning. Changing my address and stuff. Can I catch up with you at lunch?"

He nodded as if pleased with her answer. "Sounds good."

"Okay." She stood with a renewed energy that would be helpful in getting the errands done quickly.

They emptied their plates, and Hunter left. Felicity spotted Jameson at the information board and stepped up beside him.

"Hey." Well, she knew she wanted to talk to him, but she didn't really know where to begin.

"Sorry about this morning," Jameson rubbed the back of his head, tousling his hair. "I shouldn't make any assumptions before I've had caffeine."

Felicity chuckled, thankful they could apologize, forgive, and forget. "Thanks for being concerned about me, but I'm doin' okay now."

Jameson wrapped an arm around her shoulder and pulled her in for a quick hug. "I know. You're always better off than I assume. I'm proud of you, and I'm glad you're here."

"Me too. You said I'd like it here. I'm kind of sad I didn't come here sooner."

"You and me both." He looked over his shoulder as if checking to see if anyone was paying attention to them. He spoke low, and his eyes begged for truth. "Is there something going on between you and Hunter?"

Felicity turned her attention to the board on the wall, unable to look Jameson in the eye while talking about her dating life or lack of. "I don't know. Maybe?"

"If you don't know, that's a problem. A man should always be upfront about that."

"Do you tell all of your first dates you'll call them later?" she asked.

"No. I do if I really intend to call them."

She patted his shoulder. "Good boy. Just checking."

"Do you like him?" he asked.

"I do. He asked me to come out on the ranch with him today."

Jameson's eyes widened slightly. "Really? That's new."

She grinned. Knowing Hunter didn't make a habit of asking women to spend time on the ranch with him made her feel special. "Does he date a lot?"

"Not that I've ever known about. Come to think of it, I don't think I've seen him talk to a woman other than the ones who live here."

"I'm not going to promise to update you on how things are going. I'd like some space to figure this out on my own. That means I don't need your help."

"Sheesh. Tell me how you really feel." Jameson clutched his chest as if feigning injury.

She shoved his shoulder playfully. "You know what I mean. Butt out."

"Okay, okay. I won't ask."

"Until I tell you," she finished.

"Got it."

She patted his arm. "I've got to run. I want to get my errands taken care of before lunch so I can go out with Hunter."

She walked quickly to the exit but stopped short when she realized Hunter had driven her over for lunch. Maybe Jameson would be able to take her to her car. She pulled her phone from her pocket to check the time and saw an unread text.

Hunter: Sorry I had to run, but Laney said she'd take you to your car. She's waiting on you in the kitchen.

Another text came in just as she finished reading the first.

Hunter: Thanks for riding with me this morning.

Her smile grew so wide her cheeks ached. She wasn't sure where they were headed, but she was enjoying this new dynamic with Hunter.

Chapter Twelve

HUNTER

Hunter stood just outside the door to the main house flexing and fisting his fingers. It wasn't like he could take back his invitation or that he even wanted to. All he had to do was eat lunch and then spend the rest of the day with Felicity beside him.

Appealing? Yes.

Terrifying? Definitely.

The words had just slipped out. One minute he was trying and failing at idle conversation, the next he was thinking about how he didn't want to get up and go back to work, and the words just came out.

Asher parked his truck beside Hunter's. Walking in behind his attention-seeking cousin would guarantee he could sneak in unnoticed.

He'd call himself a chicken later. Right now, he needed to use the distraction to his advantage.

"Hey, Casanova!" Asher blurted as he ascended the porch stairs.

"Who?"

"You know, lover boy. Haley said you were making heart eyes at Felicity this morning."

Hunter frowned. "I was not."

"Haley has a sense for these things. I trust her. She said you've been giving the new girl longing looks since she got here. Have you kissed her yet?"

"Haley? No, I haven't kissed your wife."

Asher chuckled. "Felicity!"

Forget the distraction. Hunter needed to exit this conversation. He opened the door and walked into the meeting room. Hopefully, Asher wouldn't follow. "I'm not kissing and telling with you. Ask your wife."

"Are you saying Haley knows? Would Felicity have told her?" Asher prodded.

To be fair, Hunter knew he was an easy target for his cousin's jokes. He still didn't want to be a part of the antics. "Sounds like somebody has kissing on the brain."

"You better believe it." Asher craned his neck to scan the room. "Speaking of kissing, where's my wife?"

"Check the office," Hunter offered.

They both spotted Haley and Felicity across the room at the same time. Haley hugged a clipboard to her chest, and Felicity nodded at whatever Haley was saying.

Asher slapped a hand on Hunter's back. "See ya."

Hunter stepped up to the washing station, but he watched Felicity out of the corner of his eye. He probably wasn't subtle, but the draw he felt toward her wasn't subtle either.

Asher captured Haley's attention by interrupting her mid-sentence and dipping her into a dramatic kiss. He'd always been one to make a scene. The guy should have gone into the entertainment industry.

Felicity turned away and pinched her lips between her teeth, obviously embarrassed by the spectacle.

Hunter appreciated that she wasn't showy. All the things he liked about her were subtle. Her downplayed beauty, her eagerness to help, her quiet understanding. She drew his attention every time they were in the same room together, and she didn't have to scream and shout to get it.

After washing up, he worked his way toward Felicity. She hung back while the guests formed the beginning of the serving line, and he took his place beside her.

"Hey. How has your day been?" What else could he start with besides small talk?

"Busy," she replied, but her smile told him it was a fulfilling kind of busy. "It's a lot of work moving and settling into a new job. Even on my day off, I like to keep up with the things going on here, and there's always something."

"That's for sure."

She tucked her shoulders in and gave him a closed-lip smile. "I like that there are so many people. It's like I'm never far from a friend."

"That's true I guess. It looks like the women have adopted you."

"I guess so. Is it bad that I'm really happy about that?"

"No. If you're looking for friends, they're a great place to start."

They inched through the serving line, and Hunter chose the seat beside Felicity again. He noticed she'd been smiling easier lately, and the expression completely transformed her persona. It was almost as if she'd been asleep when she first came here, and now, she'd awoken.

They listened to the conversations bumping back and forth across the table as they ate. He cleaned his plate before her, but he didn't stand. Usually, he got his orders and got back to work, but he could see the advantages of hanging around when she was sitting beside him.

When a few people started leaving the table, he asked in a low tone, "Is there anything you want to see today?"

"I don't know what there is to see. I guess I'd like to see anything since I only got a hasty tour when I got here."

He'd spent the morning gassing up the vehicles and working on the four-wheeler Asa had gotten Jacob. Hunter looked at the grease stains on his shirt. Hopefully, he didn't smell like gasoline or grease.

She rested a hand on his arm, seeming undeterred by the black stains. "Oh, if it's okay with you, I'd like to maybe steer clear of the horses."

"I can do that. I'm pretty caught up today, so we can just ride around until you see something you like."

Her brows rose. "In your truck, right?"

"Cowboys don't always have to ride horses."

She relaxed, but her gaze darted around as the wheels in her head turned. "I think someone mentioned a creek or a river or something."

"Bluestone Creek or Blackwater River?"

"You pick."

"You ready?" he asked.

She picked up her plate and stood. "Lead the way."

On the way out, he tried to block out the overbearing thought that everyone in the room was watching them. Everyone else probably didn't care about them, but he didn't want to be the center of attention in any situation.

When they stepped outside and the noise of the meeting room fell away, he felt like he could breathe again. The weather was as mild as he could have hoped for, and he wondered when his luck for the day would run out. He hadn't gotten into a fight before breakfast, Felicity had agreed to spend the day with him, and the sun was shining. There wasn't much more he could ask for in his off time.

In the truck, Felicity looked from one side to the other, slowly taking in everything around her. "So, what do you do out here?"

"Whatever needs to be done to keep things running. Tractors always need maintenance, someone has to check the fences regularly, we have to keep an eye on the herd to make sure none of them are sick or injured, calves need to be tagged and wormed. Lots of things that aren't very interesting."

"They can get sick?" she asked.

"Yeah. We can handle some things on our own, like antibiotics, but overall herd health is something you have to keep an eye on."

"That *is* interesting." She moved to the edge of the seat and leaned forward to get a better view out the windshield. "Wow, this place is huge. It didn't seem so big when I first got here."

"It's a few thousand acres, and there are some parts that are hard to get to, like crossing the river."

They rode in silence for a while. Felicity seemed captivated by the landscape, and he let her take it all in.

When they reached the place he'd wanted her to see, he parked and pointed to the slow-flowing creek. It was wider than he would consider a creek, but since it wasn't as wide as the connecting river, it had been deemed a creek long before he'd come around.

"How do you get any work done out here?" she asked.

"I don't work out by the creek a lot. At least not this part, but this is the best place to just sit around." He pointed to a nearby boulder that was as large as his truck. "I told Noah about this spot when we were kids. He's been bringing Camille here for years."

Felicity rested a hand on her heart. "That's so sweet."

"Super romantic. Are you surprised I thought of it?" he asked.

She chuckled. "I'm not. You're a softie."

"You can't tell anyone." He found himself leaning in and didn't want to fight the urge to close the space between them.

"I'll keep your secret," she whispered.

He looked out the windshield at the creek. Bringing her here was a good idea. "Let me show you the best spot."

He walked around the front of the truck to get her door, but she was already out of the truck and checking the place out.

Jerking his head downstream, he held out a hand to her. "This way."

She slipped her hand into his without hesitating, linking their fingers together like two gears shifting into place, and the acceptance in that gesture caused a change in his soul. It was like two broken pieces fit themselves back together and fused into a whole again.

They walked through the tall grass on the bank to the big rock, and he helped her climb up. The top was flat and slightly angled toward the creek providing a perfect place to relax and watch.

She stretched out on the rock, and he did the same beside her. He rested one arm behind his head and stretched the other out toward her, allowing her to rest her head on his arm instead of the hard rock.

She lay back and closed her eyes. "This place is perfect."

He agreed. Perfect for escaping. Perfect for being alone. Perfect for getting to know someone you desperately wanted to spend your time with. Except he had no idea what people talked about when they were alone.

Moments ticked by, and he stared up at the sky trying to figure out how to do this.

Finally, she turned to him, and the gentleness in her eyes had his muscles relaxing against the hard rock at his back.

"Are you as nervous as I am?" she asked.

Hunter gave a deep chuckle. "Yeah."

"I'm nervous because you feel important."

Hunter frowned. "You can relax then. I'm not important."

She grinned and turned her face to the sky. "Agree to disagree." She closed her eyes and asked, "What do you do in the evenings, when the work is done?"

"Read the Farmer's Almanac."

Felicity laughed, bright and full of joy. Then, her expression settled back into one of confusion. "Dawn and I lived together for a long time. I'm not used to being alone yet."

He didn't remember what it was like to live with someone. He'd been on his own since he was fifteen.

"Even before we lived together, we were inseparable. We grew up together. Her mom—my aunt—helped out sometimes when my mom wasn't around."

"So you were friends," he said, assuming more than asking.

"Not always. Dawn was a liar. She lied about everything. It was her first reaction. Even when it didn't matter, she lied. After being around her so much, I started questioning everything. Not just her, but it was like I didn't know what trust or honesty really was."

Hunter reached for her hand, and she squeezed it without turning to look at him.

"I know what it's like to not have faith in anyone. I went through a phase where I pushed everyone away. My mom left, then my dad left, and I just knew everyone would leave, and I decided I didn't need them anyway."

"Your aunt and uncle never left you," she pointed out.

"I know that now, but back then, I just knew that no one wanted me. I thought that meant they were only helping me out because they felt sorry for me."

"I can tell you right now, that isn't true."

"Try telling that to a fifteen-year-old hothead. Looking back, it was a good thing I got hurt."

She raised up onto her elbows and looked down at him. "Why would you say that?"

"They saved me and didn't give up on me."

He waited for the pity look. It always came at some point when he talked about what happened. Not that he ever talked about it if he could help it. Usually, it was only doctors who wanted to know his medical history. Anyone else could pack sand.

But the pity look never came. Instead, pride spread across her face in a smile.

"I'm glad," she said quietly.

"Me too. Now, at least. Back then, I pushed them away as fast as I could. Anita found out about the scars I already had from my dad while she was helping me, but she didn't bring it up. There wasn't anything she could do anyway. Actually, she'd been protecting me for years, and I was too stupid to see it."

"How?"

"She would ask me to help her until it was late at night. That helped the most. I either slept on the couch in the main house living room or my dad was asleep by the time I got home."

"What happened?" Felicity asked. There wasn't a hesitation or uncertainty in her question. She knew that if she asked, he would tell her.

"Wild dogs."

That was always his explanation. No one needed to know about the fire of the teeth tearing his skin, the nightmares that had kept him up for years, or the times he'd prayed for an end.

Felicity was still looking down at him, and he couldn't think about anything but happiness right now. The pain of the past felt like a lost dream.

"They told me you saved Lucas," she said.

He didn't know what to say to that. A few people had praised him for his heroic sacrifice, but they would have done the same. He hadn't had a choice.

"My dad had taken everything from Silas and Anita. I couldn't let them lose their son."

Felicity's eyes turned glassy, and a single tear fell down her cheek before she wiped it away. "It wasn't your fault. You didn't deserve to be abused or left."

Hunter quirked his mouth to one side. The expression made the scarring on his face more obvious, but with Felicity, he didn't avoid it. "I could say the same about you. Getting let down doesn't give you a free pass to give up. That's what Anita taught me."

Felicity's head tilted, and she looked at him as if she didn't recognize him. But that's what she'd done. She'd been let down time and time again, and she was strong enough to keep tackling life as fast as it came at her.

"I wish I'd handled it more like you," Hunter said. "I pushed everyone away. I guess if I had a heart, I wouldn't be alone."

Felicity shook her head. "You're not alone anymore."

"Don't feel sorry for me. I'm fine. I handled it, and I'm still pushing through every day. I don't want to be your next project."

She smiled and laid back against the rock, resting her head on his arm once again. "It's a good thing I don't want to help you. Actually, I wish I were more like you. I guess you could say you've inspired me to be stronger."

"Well, that's never happened before," Hunter said.

She rolled toward him, stopping with her face only inches from his. Her body was flush against his side, and he forced a deep breath into his lungs.

"Can we see something else?" she asked.

Hunter nodded, barely registering her question, since he couldn't focus on any one thing. His gaze roamed her face and finally came to a stop on her eyes. The pupils were so dilated, the amber rings of the irises were almost invisible.

"Will you bring me here again sometime?"

He nodded again, still unsure if he could form words when she was so close. He wasn't sure if he could deny her anything she requested at this point.

He'd never bent to anyone in his life, but Felicity was about to bring him to his knees.

Chapter Thirteen

FELICITY

Felicity paced in her cabin. It was fifteen steps from one wall to the other, and she'd memorized every creak in the old wood.

He was probably asleep. *She* should be asleep. Who was she kidding? It was barely nine at night. They weren't twenty anymore, but they weren't ancient either.

She slipped into her shoes and grabbed her coat as she walked outside. Every warning she'd heard from the Harding family about the dangers of roaming the ranch at night flooded back to her, but she couldn't seem to care at the moment. Her one-track mind was stuck on Hunter and the question she had for him.

She checked over both shoulders as she stepped onto Hunter's porch, unsure of which night creatures might be waiting to sneak up on her. She stared at the door, chewing her lip, working up the nerve to knock.

How could she possibly ask him what she needed to? He'd think she was crazy.

Before she got the courage to knock, the door opened, startling her out of her internal struggle.

Hunter pulled the hem of a gray T-shirt over his torso. "What are you doing here? What's wrong?" His gaze searched her face before scanning the open ranch behind her.

She reached out and placed a calming hand on his chest. "Everything is fine. I just had something to ask you."

He stepped out of the doorway. "Come in."

His cabin was almost a mirror of her own, and she smiled at the familiarity. There were no decorations and minimal furniture.

He placed a gentle hand on the small of her back, guiding her to the couch while he took his seat in the nearby recliner. She fidgeted on the couch, and he seemed to be on edge as well. He leaned forward, propping his elbows on his knees.

"I could have come to you. You can call me anytime."

Felicity studied her hands clasped in her lap. "I know. I've just been thinking, and I couldn't sleep."

"What did you want to ask me?" he questioned with thinly veiled unease.

She took a deep breath and decided to just tell him everything. "I had a dream last night. It was more like a memory, and it made me think about something you said last week. I said I'd never needed anyone before, and you asked if I was sure about that."

Hunter's attention fell to the floor, then the fireplace, and everywhere but on her.

"I was injured a long time ago. Some people who knew Dawn attacked me. I had broken bones and bruises all over. I remember waking up in the hospital, but I don't know how I got there. I've never been able to piece it together. I've been having the same dream about that night for years, and last night, something different happened."

"Someone showed up to help you before your face got beaten in?" he asked, his tone harsh and angry.

"It was you. In the dream, I could hear someone saying my name, and it was your voice. I thought it was just because we've been spending more time together and that I was somehow integrating you into my dream, but it felt real."

He was looking at the floor, and she couldn't catch her breath.

"Hunter, look at me."

He lifted his head, and she knew the answer before she asked the question.

"Were you there? Did you save me?"

He nodded, but his face grew pale. "I'm sorry. I'm sorry I didn't get to you sooner."

"What were you doing there?" She'd been picking up groceries at the discount store when they'd attacked her from behind. She'd lost before she even knew she was in the fight.

"I'd met up with Asa that night, and I was on my way home." He linked his shaky hands and rested them behind his head.

"And you saw them? You saw me?"

"I called the police and they showed up at the hospital. They interviewed me twice."

Felicity huffed. "You mean they accused you?"

"Sort of," he admitted.

She stood in a rush. "Why didn't you tell me?"

He got to his feet and pushed a hand through his hair. "It didn't matter who helped you. All that mattered was that you got the help you needed."

"It does matter! I can't believe I never knew."

He put his hands on her arms and looked her in the eye. "I didn't want you to look at me like you owed me something. I wanted you to want me for me, and not because I helped you."

Felicity gasped. He wanted her to want him.

He huffed and paced a few steps to the right before turning and walking back.

"And I don't know that I even want you to want me. How could I want that for you when you deserve more than me?"

Felicity stared at him, unable to form words. She'd been looking for the person who'd saved her for years. There had been no information at the hospital. No trace. And now he was here, and Hunter was the man who had given her a second chance at life.

If misunderstood had a human form, it was Hunter Harding. The man who gave freely and silently of himself was ridiculed in the streets and mocked behind his back. Injustice burned hot within her, and it needed a release.

Hunter looked afraid, but she had never been more certain of anything in her life.

She wanted Hunter. With all of her heart.

Slowly, she raised her hand to his face. He turned to hide the scarred side, but she gently placed her fingertips on his jaw and turned his face. He didn't look her in the eye once as she bared the marked side.

The line wasn't clean. It was a slash of color and raised skin that stood out against the hard lines of his face. It ran up from his jaw through his beard but veered just under his eye and stopped near his temple. It was a mark she'd memorized by now—a part of Hunter just as much as the bright green of his eyes.

He let her look at the scar—the one everyone else gawked at and whispered over. Did they know about the others hidden beneath his shirt?

She grazed her fingertips over the changed skin. How could something so horrible be so beautiful?

She covered his other cheek with her hand and turned his face to hers. Finally, he looked at her, and her heart wanted to break at the sadness in his eyes.

With a hand on his shoulder, she pulled him down to her and lifted onto her toes. Her lips met his in a second when time stood still. It was a lightning bolt, a flash of awakening, and the moment when her heart and mind were in accord. This man was different, but he was the same as her in all the ways that mattered.

Before her breathing resumed, Hunter's strong arms wrapped around her, pulling her so tight against his chest that she abandoned hope for that breath.

His mouth began to move against hers, hungry and understanding. It was hard and needy, yet soft and assuring.

She may have initiated the kiss, but now Hunter had taken control. It was wild like her heart. His hands tightened on her hips, and every movement of his lips against hers promised that her heart and soul would never be the same again.

She would never be alone. Neither of them would. They had each other now.

Chapter Fourteen

FELICITY

The next morning, Felicity lay in bed grinning like a love-struck teenager. She'd been nervous about confronting Hunter, but every inkling of trepidation had dissipated since their conversation.

And that kiss. He'd set her heart on fire, and she could vividly recall every move he'd made. The places where he'd held her still tingled.

They hadn't talked much after that but only because the stress of worrying over her question all day had her yawning, and he'd walked her home. He'd kissed her again in front of her door.

Her heart felt free, and it was worth taking a morning minute to bask in the comfort. For the first time since Dawn's death, Felicity was happy.

A knock on the door interrupted her daydreams. Flinging the covers back, she rushed out of bed and swiped at her hair. It was a lost cause, unless she wanted to keep the person at the door waiting.

"Coming!" She grabbed a robe from the back of her door on the way to the front of the cabin.

She'd hoped it might be Hunter, but she was equally surprised to see Jameson on the porch looking bright eyed and bushy tailed before seven in the morning.

"Hey. Sorry. Were you asleep?" he asked.

"No. I was just being lazy about getting out of bed. Come in."

He made himself at home in the kitchen, pulling up a chair at the small, round table. "You doing all right?"

"Yep. You want coffee?" she asked as she opened a cabinet.

"Why not. I have some good news, and I wanted to tell you first. Well, second. I talked to Silas and Anita last night."

"Good news is always welcome. Lay it on me."

"I got a job offer."

Felicity turned from the coffee maker with wide eyes. "A job? But you already have two."

"True, but this one would actually replace the job here. That's why I needed to talk to the Hardings first."

"You're leaving?" She didn't mean to sound accusing, but it was her first reaction. She'd just gotten close to him, and she was selfishly sad to lose him again.

"It wouldn't be far. Just back to Wolf Creek Ranch." He pointed to the right with his thumb as if the ranch was just outside.

"Oh, well that's good. Why would you want to go back there? You don't like it here?"

"It's a promotion. I love working and living here, but the job Mr. Chambers offered me is a foreman position."

"Is that like a boss?" she asked.

"It's like a big boss. I always got along well with him, and now that Henry Bowman is retiring, Mr. Chambers wants me to come back as foreman."

"Wow. That sounds important. I can't believe he sought you out. You didn't even have to apply?"

Jameson shook his head. "Nope."

Pride swelled in her chest, and she left the coffee pot to embrace her brother. "This is great! I'm guessing you'd live there."

"I would, but like I said, it's not far."

She hugged his shoulders tight, realizing again that her little brother was grown and a respected employee by all who knew him. "You live a hundred yards away, and I hardly see you now. I'm gonna miss you."

"I'll miss you too, sis. Like I said, I won't be far."

She released him and went back to the coffee. "Will you still work at the fire station?"

"I'm not sure yet. I really haven't made up my mind about any of this. I talked to Silas and Anita last night to make sure they wouldn't be shorthanded if I did decide to go, but I also wanted their advice. They've been like parents to me."

Felicity watched the first trickling of coffee falling into the carafe and tried not to get teary-eyed. She'd be forever thankful to the Hardings for taking in her brother, and now, herself. She and her brother both needed that positive relationship.

"They told me to pray about it too. I don't have to give Mr. Chambers an answer until next week."

She grabbed two to-go mugs from the cabinet and put sugar and creamer in hers. "You liked him when you worked there before, right?"

"Oh yeah. He's as good as Silas and Anita have been to me. Henry said he'd stick around long enough to train me, but I know he's ready to retire."

Another knock sounded at the door, and she set Jameson's coffee in front of him before going to answer it.

This time, she was happy to see Hunter's face. He even wore that handsome smile she adored.

She could get used to a happy Hunter in her life.

Wiping a hand over her still messy hair, she hoped the tangles weren't noticeable. "Good morning."

"Morning. I wanted to see if you wanted a ride to the main house."

"I'd love that. Let me just kick my brother out."

Jameson stepped up behind her, holding the Styrofoam cup of coffee. "I see how it is."

"Sorry. I didn't know you had company," Hunter said, retreating into that reserved state she knew so well.

"He was just leaving." She laid a guiding hand on her brother's back to push him out the door. "Bye."

"I get it. I get it. Sheesh." He stopped on the porch beside Hunter. "Hey, I was just telling Felicity I got a job offer at Mr. Chambers' place. I might not be around here much longer. Keep an eye on her, will you?"

Felicity stuck her hands on her hips. "I don't need a babysitter."

Hunter jerked his head toward her. "What she said, but I don't mind keeping an eye on her."

Hunter gave her a playful wink, and her stomach did a flip. She wasn't sure how he did that to her—made her feel like she was on a roller coaster with a simple wink—but she loved it.

Jameson waved a hand over his head as he stepped off the porch and headed to his truck parked in front of his cabin. "See you later."

Hunter turned back to her with a grin. "No fists this time."

"Progress," she said as she laid a hand on his chest. Lifting up onto her toes, she kissed him quickly. "You mentioned breakfast?"

He looked down to her robe. "I'll hang out while you get dressed."

"Come in and have a cup of coffee. I just made it."

Hunter stepped inside and closed the door behind him. She tried not to hover, wondering what he thought about being in her cabin.

She rushed through changing clothes and brushing her hair, and she even swiped a light dusting of makeup on her face. The dark circles under her eyes were beginning to lighten, but it would take more than one night of good sleep to make them disappear.

Ten minutes later, she joined Hunter in the kitchen where she found him nursing a cup of coffee. He held out his arm for her, and she looped hers through it. He led her to his truck and opened the passenger side door for her. The Queen of England would be jealous of this courteous treatment.

When Hunter took his place in the driver's seat, he started the truck and reached over to take her hand. He linked his fingers with hers and held on tight.

He put the truck in reverse and looked over his shoulder. "I actually wanted to see if you had plans tonight. Asher and I are playing at Barn Sour."

"Will you sing?"

"Nah. That's Asher's job."

"I'd love to hear you sing," she said quietly.

He lifted her hand and placed a soft kiss on her knuckles. "I will. But not for everyone. Just you."

Her cheeks grew warm, and she leaned over to whisper in his ear, "Thank you."

He didn't say anything else, just kept his eyes on the path ahead and grinned.

***

Hunter and Asher rushed through supper that night. Felicity's stomach was a ball of excitement, and her appetite was nowhere in sight.

Despite his hurry, Hunter asked about her day and let her do most of the talking while he scarfed down a cheeseburger and fries. When his plate was clean, he kissed her on the cheek.

"Sorry I have to leave so soon."

Felicity waved a hand, still a little lightheaded from the rush of Hunter's public display of affection. "No worries. I'm riding with Noah and Camille."

A loud whistle drew their attention to the exit where Asher and Haley were waving Hunter to hurry up. He squeezed her hand quickly before letting it go.

"That is so cute!" Jade squealed across the table.

"What?" Levi asked. "What's cute?"

"Hunter and Felicity are sweet on each other."

Levi's face didn't scrunch up in a disgusted expression the way Felicity expected. Instead, the little boy's eyes widened. "Hunter has a wife?"

Jade laughed. "Not a wife. A girlfriend. That comes before wife."

Though they hadn't actually had a conversation to define the relationship, she hoped she was Hunter's girlfriend. Something told her he wouldn't mind the label.

"I have a girlfriend," Levi said. "But I thought grownups had husbands and wives."

Aaron tousled his son's hair. "Don't worry about husbands and wives, or girlfriends, for that matter. You definitely don't have a girlfriend."

"I do so!" Levi argued. "Willow always sits by me in Sunday School, and she lets me play with her hair."

Laney kept her attention on her plate as she whispered, "Playing with her hair. He's got it bad."

"Got what?" Levi asked.

"Cooties," Lucas answered. "Girls have cooties."

"What's that? Is it contagious?" Levi asked, a look of worry covering his earlier excitement.

"It's catching," Lucas explained. "Girls don't grow out of them until they get older and it's safe to ask them to be your girlfriend."

Aaron elbowed Lucas. "Stop telling my kid lies." He turned to Levi. "What your uncle means is that you're too young to have a girlfriend, and little girls don't have a contagious disease."

Levi's shoulders sagged in relief. "That's good. I kissed Willow on the cheek last week, and I thought I was infested."

"You what?" Jade asked, her pitch rising.

"Definitely infested," Lucas said. "Or is it infected?"

"It could be either, I think, but that's not the point," Jade said. "Levi, please don't be kissing girls in Sunday School."

"What about on the playground?" he asked.

Felicity laughed. "You've got a heartbreaker on your hands."

Jade sighed. "They grow up so fast." She turned to Levi. "Why don't you just worry about having fun without the kissing for now."

"I'll try," Levi said.

Camille rose to her feet a few seats down. "Come on, buddy. Let's find you some dessert."

Levi jumped up and followed his aunt to the kitchen. Felicity picked up her own plate and returned it to the serving counter before slipping into the kitchen.

Mama Harding was already busy washing dishes.

"Can I help?" Felicity asked.

"Oh, no. I've got things handled here. Y'all go on."

"You don't want to go hear the boys play? I can stay here and take care of things." Though she didn't want to miss Hunter playing, she felt bad that his aunt and uncle were stuck cleaning up while everyone else went out and had a good time.

"I've heard them both play and sing before. My boys know I love them."

Felicity smiled. "They sure do. Jameson told me he talked to you about the new job offer. Are you really okay with him leaving?"

"We are. This is a great opportunity for him. He's still so young, and there are lots more older, seasoned workers who could qualify for that position. It's not something we could ask him to pass up. We'll miss him, but taking a job like that while he's still young might save his body a lot of backbreaking work hours."

"That's a good point. The people around here work hard."

"And they pay for it later in life. It's why Silas is happy to let the younger men do the heavy lifting around here. He's earned some rest time."

"Who else worked here when Silas was working the ranch?" Felicity asked.

"We've had quite a few workers come and go. Many ranch hands are on the rougher side, and they didn't all appreciate our Christian values. We tried to be a good influence, but I could tell which ones felt stifled by our faith."

"That's a shame. I hope you were able to influence a few of them."

"Oh, we did. Butch was around for a while, and he was one we couldn't reach."

"Butch?" Felicity asked.

"Hunter's dad. He had money on his mind, and it clouded his judgment." Mama Harding looked up from the pan she was washing. "Thankfully, Hunter didn't turn out that way. He has always had a good head on his shoulders, even if Butch tried to tear him down."

"I know what you mean."

Mama Harding looked back to the soapy water but didn't resume washing the dish. "I know your folks weren't kind either, but we're blessed to have you here. And thank you for seeing through Hunter's mask."

"It's a shame that everyone can't see it," Felicity said.

"Hunter never needed the approval of the world. All he needs is one."

Felicity wrapped her arms around Mama Harding's shoulders. "Thank you."

"Anytime, dear. You go on."

Felicity walked back into the meeting room and found Noah and Camille talking to Laney.

Camille waved Felicity over as soon as she spotted her. "Hey, Laney is riding with us too. Micah had something come up."

"Perfect. I won't be the third wheel," Felicity said as they made their way outside.

On the ride to Barn Sour, Felicity had the overwhelming feeling of being surrounded by friends. Most of her friends had come and gone over the years, leaving only Dawn, her flesh and blood, as her constant friend.

But being with the Hardings was different. They'd already carved out a place in her heart, and she felt immersed in their home, friendship, and family.

Barn Sour was an older building outside of town. She'd heard of it before, but this was her first time here, and she was glad it was with a handful of friends.

Inside, the restaurant and bar had a weathered atmosphere. The wooden floors and tables were clean, but every surface was scratched and dented. Yet, the place was bustling with conversations and laughter above the background songs from the jukebox.

Hunter and Asher stood next to the bar talking to a woman wearing a half apron and a bright smile. She looked to be somewhere in her mid-forties, but her blonde-streaked curly hair gave her a younger look to match her joyous expression.

Felicity caught Hunter's eye as she sat at a booth with Camille, Noah, and Laney. Hunter and Asher came by to say a quick hello before their set. Everyone left at the table ordered drinks as the live music filled the air, sending an awakening current through the patrons.

Within minutes, the open area in front of the slightly-raised stage was teeming with couples dancing and swinging to the music.

As he'd promised, Hunter didn't sing, but his talent on the guitar was fascinating. Playing the chords seemed to come as easy as breathing to him as they moved from one song to the next.

Camille and Haley convinced Felicity that it was easy to learn to line dance. It wasn't as easy as they claimed, but she had a blast tripping over her own feet as well as everyone else's.

She looked up at Hunter each time she stumbled, but embarrassment never came. When he smiled back at her, she was laughing at herself and having a good time doing it.

Jameson danced with a smiling woman nearby. The happiness on his face was everything she'd always wanted for her little brother. The kid who'd consumed her childhood and teen years was growing into a man she was proud to call her flesh and blood.

Felicity would miss her brother, but she had a bigger family now.

Chapter Fifteen

HUNTER

When their set was over, Hunter and Asher loaded their equipment into Asher's truck. He and Haley usually left early and took the equipment back to the main house.

Hunter stepped off the stage after he'd cleaned up unnoticed behind Asher's fanfare. The guy drew attention to himself like moths to a flame, and Hunter only agreed to play in front of strangers because Asher drew the attention to himself.

Felicity stood off to the side of the open area in front of the stage, playing the wallflower part perfectly.

He wove his way through the mass of people and took his place beside her. For a quiet moment, they watched the others dancing. Was he supposed to ask her to dance?

She turned to him, flipping her ponytail over a shoulder. "You did great."

"Thanks. It's not much, but it keeps the people around here entertained."

She pointed to the dancers swinging their partners to "Dixieland Delight." "Do you do that?"

"Dance?" Of course she wanted to dance. He'd avoided the touching and bumping into each other scene at Barn Sour his entire life, but he'd enter the crowd if Felicity wanted him to do it.

"Yeah."

"I haven't before," he admitted.

"Me either. I looked like a stumbling baby deer out there."

"I liked it—watching you have fun."

"I liked watching you play, but I think I'll stick to the sidelines from now on. I came too close to twisting an ankle at the end there."

Hunter reached for her hand and linked his fingers between hers. "I'll dance with you if you want to."

"Nah. I think I'm done for the evening."

He leaned in to be heard above the louder song that had just begun. "You want to find a table?"

"Sure."

Felicity led them to the table Noah, Camille, Laney, and Felicity had occupied earlier in the evening. She asked a waitress for a refill of water, and Hunter ordered one for himself.

"This is amazing. The two of you sounded great." Her eyes were wide and bright in the yellow-tinged bar lights.

"Thanks. Things don't get rowdy here until after nine, and they've been letting us play since we were teenagers. It gave me something to do when I was stuck inside recovering for weeks."

His phone vibrated in his pocket, and he pulled it out. "This is Haley."

Felicity waved a hand for him to answer it. "Asher probably forgot something."

"Hello."

"Hey. Are you with Felicity?" Haley asked.

Her tone was more serious than usual, but Hunter tried not to show his concern.

"Yeah. You need to talk to her?"

"No. Can the two of you come to the main house? It's kind of important."

Hunter made eye contact with Felicity and nudged his head toward the door. "Okay."

"And don't stop at your cabins. Just come straight here," Haley added.

"Got it," Hunter disconnected the call as he stood and reached for Felicity's hand. "Haley wants us to come to the main house."

Felicity took his hand and kept a brisk pace. "Is everything okay?"

"I'm not sure. She just said don't stop at our cabins."

On the ride back to the ranch, Hunter held Felicity's hand in the darkness that filled the cab. He had a twisting gut feeling that this had something to do with Cain, and if Haley knew about it, then it also had to do with the ranch.

They hadn't exactly been trying to keep Felicity's location a secret, thinking Cain would just leave her alone now. It was unlikely she had anything the guy wanted now that he'd taken her dog and Dawn's expensive earrings. The diamonds were probably long gone by now.

When Hunter and Felicity arrived at the main house, the meeting room was quiet. Most of the family was still at Barn Sour, and the guests were probably in their rooms for the night.

"She's probably in the office," Hunter said as he toed off his boots at the door.

The office light was on, and Haley sat in front of a laptop on the desk. Micah, Asher, Silas, and Anita all stood behind her.

Haley waved Hunter and Felicity over. "Come here."

The rest of the family made room for Hunter and Felicity, and the silence in the room was threatening to choke the breath from his lungs.

Haley pointed to the screen. "After Laney was attacked last year, I started building a surveillance system around the ranch. Nothing major, but I wanted to have a warning if we had any more trouble. We needed to be prepared to protect the family and the guests."

Hunter studied the grid of videos on the screen. He recognized a few of the scenes, but some were parts of the wooded areas of the ranch, and it was impossible to distinguish the exact location.

"There are also perimeter alarms near the entrance and the cabins. I get notifications on my phone and computer when something trips the alarm. It's usually an animal, but tonight I got a notification, and it was a person."

Haley enlarged one of the video screens. It was dark, but a white glow lit some of the trees the way game camera footage looked at night.

"It starts here," Haley said as a man wearing overalls and boots walked through the woods in the video.

Hunter froze. The sight of the familiar form sent a chill down his spine that had him reaching for Felicity, pulling her close to his side.

"It's like seeing a ghost," Mama Harding whispered.

The bright white light did make the man look ethereal, but Butch Harding had disappeared without a trace over fifteen years ago. He might as well have been dead ever since.

"Who is it?" Felicity asked as Haley pulled up the next screen.

They all watched as the man walked through the path of another surveillance camera.

"My dad," Hunter said.

Felicity stiffened beside him and inched closer. She knew a fraction of the damage that Butch Harding was capable of inflicting.

"He's got a lot of nerve coming back here," Micah said.

"This is why I didn't want you to go to the cabins," Haley said as she pointed to another screen that showed a dark video of the cleared area behind the wranglers' cabins. Butch walked straight into the row of cabins and disappeared.

"We think he went in between your cabins. I'm not sure if he went in either of them or if he was just scouting, but you need to check your places tonight. See if anything is missing or looks disturbed."

"I don't think it's safe for Felicity to stay there," Hunter said.

Felicity gripped his hand, shattering the image of calm she portrayed in her silence. Her cabin was one of only two with a lock on it, since

Laney had lived there before. Micah had installed the added security when Laney's ex-boyfriend had continued to bother her.

Haley looked to Micah who seemed to be thinking with his arms crossed over his chest and a hard expression on his face. "I'd say it's not."

Haley looked up at Felicity from her seat. "Better safe than sorry. Asher and I think you should stay at our place until we get this figured out. We need to let the police know, and I'd like to put up some better security around the cabins."

Hunter exhaled a relieved breath. He'd feel much better if Felicity stayed at Asher and Haley's place. They'd recently built a house on the southern edge of the ranch, and Felicity would be protected by more than an old wooden door.

Felicity looked from one Harding to the next, gauging their expressions. "I'd really appreciate that, but you're newlyweds, and you'll have a baby soon. I don't want to be in the way."

Haley stood and wrapped her arms around Felicity. The baby bump was a reminder between them. "Don't think another thing about it. We'd love to have you."

"Yeah, we subscribe to the more the merrier mindset," Asher said.

"I'll let Asa know," Micah said, pulling his phone from his pocket. "He'll want a report and a copy of the video."

"I'll make a copy for him," Haley said as she sat back in front of the computer.

Hunter kept a hold on Felicity's hand, unwilling to let go. He wanted to keep her beside him every second. With Butch sneaking around the ranch, Felicity's safety wasn't something he could leave up to chance.

"We need to lock up the equipment," Silas said.

Asher rubbed his chin. "We changed all the places we hid keys after Butch left."

"I know, but Butch knows this place like the back of his hand. If he wanted to find the keys to anything out here, he'd have a fair advantage when he went looking," Silas pointed out.

Hunter lifted his chin. "I'll do it."

Haley looked over her shoulder. "As soon as I finish this, I'll take Felicity to her house to get some of her stuff."

Hunter lifted Felicity's hand and kissed her knuckles. He leaned close to her and whispered, "He's probably just here to steal. Don't worry about it."

Felicity's expression was guarded as she whispered back, "I know. I'll be fine."

"I'll call you when I finish and see if you still need help with anything."

Felicity looked up at him with a bravery that he expected. "Thanks, but Haley and I can probably get anything I'll need tonight in one trip. I'll get the rest later."

He stepped around her and out the door, already feeling the distance between them.

He hadn't wanted an intrusive neighbor when Felicity arrived at the ranch, but she'd slowly crept into the fortress he'd built around himself. The strange part was that he'd let her. She hadn't been bothersome like he'd expected. She'd filled the wounds his dad had created and knitted his broken pieces back together.

In the darkness of the truck, he slammed the heel of his hand into the steering wheel, releasing the pressure building in his chest. His dad had taken everything from him, and now he was taking Felicity. She was moving less than a quarter of a mile away, but it felt like the ground between them was now covered in obstacles.

The unease continued to roil in his thoughts and heart as he found new hiding places for the building and equipment keys. His dad was back, and while they knew he'd be after something, they didn't know what. The uncertainty fueled a rage in

Hunter as he drove from barn to barn locking up everything of value the ranch owned.

It was late in the night when Hunter finished his job. Felicity was probably asleep, but he sent a text hoping she'd get it in the morning.

Hunter: Good night.

He'd driven a few hundred yards toward his cabin when her reply came through.

Felicity: Can you come by? I'll meet you at the back door.

Hunter: On my way.

He wanted to see her, but the constant need to lay eyes on her was his own problem. She might not feel the same, but he was thankful that tonight they were on the same page.

He parked near Asher and Haley's back door. The flood light was on, and Felicity leaned against the railing on the back deck wrapped in a thin coat.

The invisible rope that spanned the space between them grew taut as he ascended the few stairs to the deck. Felicity greeted him with open arms, and he embraced her, holding her tight enough to feel the thumping of her heart against his chest.

"I just wanted to make sure you were all right," she whispered.

Hunter leaned back. She looked up at him with her worrisome expression shadowed by the single outdoor light. She usually wore her hair pulled back, but tonight it framed her face. He pushed a strand behind her ear and felt the softness brush over his fingers.

"I'm fine as long as you're safe."

"I doubt he's after me. You should be the one moving."

Hunter shook his head. "I'm not worried about me. He can't take anything from me except you, and that's a chance I'm not willing to take."

"He doesn't care about me. He doesn't even know about me."

"No chances," Hunter reiterated as he leaned in and sealed his lips with hers. The kiss was short and powerful. Everything he thought he'd been working toward in his life shifted.

He had a reason to keep going, a purpose for the future. He had Felicity, and everything to come felt monumental.

Awareness had his throat clogging. He was falling in love with Felicity, and everything he'd ever experienced in his life was a pale comparison to the honor of having her by his side.

Chapter Sixteen

FELICITY

Felicity threw a stick past the playground beside the main house, and Dixie sprinted after it. A few of the kids on the playground stuck their hands out to the dog as she raced past, and their giggles mixed with other raised voices. The guests with families loved Jade's activity programs for the kids that allowed them to take day trips with their spouses.

Jade stood on the other side of the playground directing pairs of children to the starting line of the obstacle course.

Dixie returned with the stick, and Felicity rubbed the dog's neck before throwing the stick again.

She spotted Hunter's truck cresting the rise leading from the stables. It was the middle of the day, and two hours before the next meal was served at the main house.

Jade pointed to the truck. "What's he doing?"

The workers seldom came in from the fields between mealtimes. Felicity shrugged and walked to the front of the house to greet him.

Grease stains covered his T-shirt, and a layer of dirt and sweat covered his face.

"Didn't expect to see you back yet," she said, hoping he'd assure her that his unexpected visit wasn't anything to worry about.

He placed a quick kiss on her cheek while keeping his dirty hands and body a safe distance away.

"Asa's on his way." Hunter looked toward the entrance to the ranch where an SUV approached. "Here he is."

"Is everything okay? Did they find out something about your dad?" she asked with mounting concern.

"He has good news."

They waited for Asa to park before walking over to greet him.

Asa's friendly grin dispelled her worries. He must really have good news. She saw him at church every Sunday, and he was always friendly, but today his happiness was elevated.

"We got him," Asa said proudly as he opened the back door of his Tahoe cruiser.

Felicity peered into the back seat and gasped. Boone sat cowering in an animal carrier that was made to fit the entire back of the vehicle.

When Boone saw her, he made his way out of the vehicle with a lot less enthusiasm than she'd expected.

"Boone!" she shouted as she wrapped her companion in her arms. With a sour face, she pulled back. "Ew. You stink."

Asa chuckled. "My vehicle will need a detailing after this, but I wanted to get him straight to you."

Felicity rubbed her hands all over the Black and Tan's filthy head and neck, but she jerked away when she saw the gashes and hairless patches. "What did he do to you?"

"Looks like we get to add animal cruelty charges to Cain's list of charges," Asa said. "Unfortunately, Boone wasn't the only one we confiscated. We're gathering evidence to hopefully put him away for a while."

"How?" she asked, hopeful that Cain would be out of her life soon.

Asa shuffled his feet, delaying. "He's fighting dogs."

"He's what?" Felicity screamed as she stood in a rush.

Dixie inched closer, curious about the new dog, but Boone stuck timidly to Felicity's side. Her playful, carefree companion had been at the mercy of a dog fighter for eight weeks. She'd prayed unfailingly the entire time, and while she was glad to have him back, it broke her heart to see the lingering effects of Cain's cruelty.

"How did you get him?" she asked in a flat tone, trying to will her heart rate to steady.

Asa crossed his arms. "Let's just say Cain messed up, and we got our opportunity."

Felicity shook her head as tears began to cloud her eyes. Her sweet Boone was home and safe. "I don't know how to thank you. This is…" She buried her nose and mouth in the crook of her elbow and squeezed her eyes closed.

Hunter extended a hand to Asa. "Thanks, man."

"Don't mention it," Asa said, shaking the hand with extra gusto. "This is a mark in the win column for all of us. I'm still looking for the earrings, but there's a good chance Cain sold them by now."

Felicity wiped her tears on her sleeve. "I don't care about the earrings." She looked up at Hunter as a thought entered her mind. "Do you think Boone can stay at the ranch? Silas and Anita didn't really agree to this when I moved in."

Hunter nodded. "They won't mind."

Dixie and Boone were now sniffing and circling each other. It might take some time for them to become friends, but this looked like a good start.

Boone had a lot of coddling in his future. Felicity had her friend back, and he was going to know how much she cared about him.

Asa chuckled. "Looks like Dixie is excited to have a friend."

"Me too," Felicity confirmed. "I'm so happy. Thank you," she said, clasping her hands at her chest.

"I was happy to help. But just so you're aware, Cain wasn't too happy about parting with him or the others." Asa pointed a thumb at Boone. "As far as we know, he hasn't made another move against you, but it's best to keep your guard up. Especially after this blow. If we disbanded his illegitimate business, he may either have more time on his hands or go looking for revenge."

Unwrapping the mind of a criminal wasn't something she'd thought about before. She'd spent years trying to figure out her addicted cousin, but this seemed different and just as dangerous. "I will. Thanks, again."

Asa clapped his hands. "I gotta run. I'll let you know if I hear anything else."

Hunter slapped a hand on his friend's shoulder. "See ya."

Felicity stepped to Hunter's side and watched Boone and Dixie slowly getting to know each other. "I can't believe they got him back."

Hunter rested an arm around her shoulders, and she didn't care that he was dirty. This was cause for celebration. "Asa's good at his job."

"What if Cain comes for him again? It wasn't like he really wanted Boone for himself, right? He just wanted to do something to hurt me because he was angry. Then he found a way to use him." She shuddered at the awful thoughts of what he could have done to Boone or the other dogs.

"I don't know," Hunter admitted. "But if he comes here, he'd better have a death wish."

Felicity rested her head on Hunter's strong shoulder. She didn't care if he was dirty or smelled as bad as Boone. "I hope it's over. I don't want anyone to get hurt."

Hunter placed a hand on her jaw and lifted her chin to look up at him. "You don't have to watch your back alone anymore. I'm always here for you."

She closed her eyes and said a silent prayer of thanks that the Lord had put Hunter in her path. She hadn't known to pray for a man who would stand beside her through everything, but that's exactly what she got, and it seemed like more than she deserved.

***

Felicity followed Maddie into Grady's Feed and Seed.

Maddie pointed. "This way," she said as she speed-walked toward the horse feed section. "Can you grab a cart? The big flatbed if there's one available."

Felicity halted and turned around to get the cart. She liked hanging out with Maddie, but it was difficult to catch her when she wasn't surrounded by hulking animals, so Felicity usually volunteered to go with Maddie to the store. They got to spend the girl time together without horses hanging around.

A shiver raced up Felicity's spine at the thought of the massive animals. Horses were pretty if seen at a distance or in one of Haley's paintings or drawings, but Felicity liked to keep a healthy distance from the stables and the horses within.

She pushed the cart to the feed section where Maddie usually shopped and found her friend staring at a massive selection of options.

"They're out of Vader's feed. Can you find Grady and ask him when they'll be getting more in?" Maddie grabbed the tag from the shelf and handed it to Felicity. "It's this one."

"Sure. Be right back."

"Great. I should have the rest loaded by then."

Felicity set out at a brisk pace, turning her head from one side to the other to look around shelving and pallets stacked with bags.

She slowed when she saw two men talking down an aisle and took an extra second to see if Grady was one of the men. Her eyes widened when she recognized Cain standing with his arms crossed over his chest and talking with the other man whose back was to her.

Unsure if Cain had spotted her, she tried to casually walk on past the opening of the aisle and stop just on the other side of it. She listened hard as the men talked. She wanted to know what Cain was up to, and the other man's stance had looked familiar, though she couldn't place him.

"I can get it. I snuck into the place not too long ago," the other man said to Cain.

Felicity covered her mouth. It was Butch, and he was talking to Cain of all people. The two people Felicity and Hunter wanted to never see again were planning something at the ranch.

"I'd do it myself, but I don't know the place like you. I want it alive," Cain specified.

"You gonna fight it?" Butch asked.

"Nah. I'll use it for practice, but not the real fights."

Butch scoffed. "Then why the big deal over this one? You can pick up any mutt off the street and watch the others tear it apart."

Felicity choked, and she covered her mouth to stifle the cough that was clogging her tight throat. She wanted to retch, and holding back her body's response to the horrific image of Cain killing dogs had her eyes watering.

She heard Cain curse her name with the vitriol of a sailor.

"She'll remember who she's talking to next time she sees me. We'd still have our kennel full if she hadn't opened her trap. Hopefully, I'll get to see the look on her face when I give it back to her in a bag."

"I have some unfinished business there myself."

"What are you doing here?" another man shouted, clearly angry.

Felicity kept her hand tight over her mouth and nose as she peeked her head around the corner to see who had joined the men. Maddie had pointed out Kent Price, one of the workers at Grady's, and Felicity knew enough to know the man had it out for Hunter for no good reason.

"We're shopping. What does it look like?" Cain growled at the intruder.

"The two of you have five seconds to get out of my store. I'm calling the police too," Kent promised.

"Last I checked, it wasn't your store," Butch taunted. "In fact, I think you probably don't have a dime left to your name after what you did to Grady's place."

"Get out!" Kent shouted.

"Fine then, be sure to tell Grady I'll take my business somewhere else," Butch said.

"Your business?" Kent seethed. "You've never paid an honest dollar for anything in your life! You're here to steal, and it ain't happening today." Kent went on cursing the two, enraged by their presence.

Cain mockingly laughed at the riled up old man. "Got it, geezer. We'll take it outside."

Felicity slipped into the next aisle as Butch and Cain headed for the door followed by a disgruntled Kent. She tried to slow her breathing. Her heart beat hard and fast, and in the silence after the men left, she could have sworn the thudding was audible.

She stuck her head past the end of the shelving and didn't see the men. In a surge of adrenaline, she wove her way through the warehouse looking for Maddie.

Felicity almost ran into her friend as they rounded a corner at the same time.

"Good grief," Maddie said, clutching her chest. "What's the rush?"

"Cain and Butch were here," Felicity whispered loudly, which defeated the purpose of the discretion, but she didn't care.

Maddie's eyes widened. "Here?"

"Yes. They were together and talking about Butch sneaking onto the ranch to take Boone."

Maddie's shoulders straightened. She'd taken a quick liking to the newest animal on the ranch, and she'd even helped clean Boone's wounds. "That's not happening."

"Right. We need to get back. Hurry."

The two sped to the register, unconcerned about Felicity's original mission to find Grady and ask him about the feed. Maddie rushed the usually chatty Loraine through the checkout, while Felicity stepped just outside the store to call Hunter. He was moving a herd today, and the hope of getting in touch with him dissipated with each passing ring.

When Hunter's voicemail picked up, she rolled the phone in her hands. What could she do? Those two needed to be stopped, but she didn't even know where they'd gone after Kent ran them off.

Kent had said he would call the police. Had he really done it? If so, they may be on their way right now, but what were the chances they would send an officer down here if Kent didn't have any claims to make other than he didn't like the men? They'd left when he told them to.

She scrolled to Asa's number in her phone and placed the call.

He answered on the second ring. "Officer Scott."

"Asa. It's me, Felicity."

"Is everything okay?"

"I don't know. I'm at Grady's with Maddie, and I overheard Cain and Butch talking."

Asa huffed, clearly unhappy to hear that the two criminals were banding together. "Butch sure makes quick work of getting into trouble."

"He told Cain he knew how to get on the ranch. He admitted to sneaking in recently." Felicity swallowed hard as a burning like acid crept up her throat. "Cain said he wanted it alive."

"Boone?" Asa asked.

"That's the only thing it could be. I just got him back, and Cain wants to take him again."

"Where are they now?"

"Kent Price ran them off. He said he was going to call the police."

"I'll confirm that. Two witnesses are better than one, as long as you both have the same statement."

"I don't know if he heard the conversation. He barged in and told them to get out."

"So Butch and Cain left the store? Do you know if they left together?"

"I don't know."

Maddie walked past with the cart followed by a teenage boy. She never accepted help loading the truck from the workers, but Felicity was glad she'd taken the offer today since they were in a hurry to get out of here.

"I'll see if Grady will let me look at the parking lot surveillance. What time did this happen?"

Felicity looked at her watch. "About seven minutes ago."

"Thanks for calling. I'll probably swing by the ranch later to get a signed statement from you. I'll let you know if we hear anything else."

Felicity headed across the parking lot to where Maddie and the boy were finishing the loading. "Thanks for everything. I really thought this stuff with Cain was over."

"Repeat offenders rarely let things go," Asa said. "It's a vicious cycle that they can't break. And I knew Cain would be mad about the dogs."

The past came rushing back to her. Each memory hit like a needle as they pricked her skin.

Her mother's second and third overdoses.

The rounds of men who came and went throughout her childhood.

Dawn's relapses, and the one that finally did her in.

The things that drugs and alcohol had cost her were stacked one on top of the next. The final price had been the lives of her mother and cousin.

"I know," she whispered. The sinking realization cut like a knife. The perfect life she'd been living at Blackwater Ranch was all crashing down.

"Listen to me." Asa's tone was stern like she'd never heard before. "We'll find them."

His words rang with truth, and Felicity remembered the kind but fiercely protective army that now stood beside her at the ranch. The "we" Asa referred to wasn't just the local police force. He'd have every able-bodied person in town on the lookout for Butch and Cain.

She wrapped up the call with Asa and climbed into Maddie's truck.

"What did he say?"

Felicity raised her chin, resolved to her role in bringing the two men to justice. "He said we'll get them."

She hadn't come here to fight, but she'd put her boots on the ground to protect her new friends.

Since moving to Blackwater Ranch, she'd been struggling to conform to a new life of freedom, leaving behind the things that had weighed her down before.

Now, she had a new purpose, and she'd fight with everything she had to protect the future from the ghosts of the past.

Chapter Seventeen

HUNTER

Hunter parked behind the main house and snuck in through the back door. Felicity would probably be in the office with Haley or in the laundry room with Laney.

He chose the path of least resistance and hoped he didn't run into anyone before he found Felicity. To top off the most grueling workday he'd had all year, he'd gotten back to his truck to find Felicity's missed calls and messages.

Butch and Cain teaming up meant Hunter and Felicity had double the trouble headed their way, and he'd rushed back to the main house to see her. If she was rattled, he'd know it by the look in her eyes.

After confirming she wasn't in the living room, he entered the back hallway and found her humming in the laundry room with Boone curled up at her feet.

The sweet sound halted with a gasp when she saw him. "Hunter, you scared me."

He closed the door behind him and closed the distance between them. Cradling her face in his dirty hands, he studied her eyes, searching for any sign of worry in their depths.

When the mounds of her cheeks lifted and shallow lines crinkled beside her eyes, the tension in Hunter's shoulders dissipated.

While Felicity's brave, assuring, and polite smiles were frequent, her carefree smiles were rare. This one was a mix of joy and relief that lit a fire in his veins that traveled to every part of his body.

He leaned down and pressed his lips to hers, breathing in her sweet smell that reminded him of summer flowers after a warm rain, a rarity in Wyoming. Her arms wound around his shoulders, pulling him closer, and a deep rumble emanated from his chest.

This was a peace like he'd never known, and the long day of back-breaking work didn't matter anymore. If he got to come home to Felicity's arms every day, he'd die a happy man.

She pulled back and hummed. "Well, hello to you too."

"I thought about you all day," he said before leaning in to kiss her cheek, then her temple.

"Waiting for the sun to go down was torture." He kissed her hairline, then her nose.

Her eyes closed, and she lifted her chin to his adorations. "I couldn't agree more."

Hunter's muscles tightened as the dread crept its way back into his happy thoughts, slowly strangling the contentment from their reunion. "Then I got your call, and I had to see you."

She wrapped her arms around his neck and buried her face between his shoulder and neck. "I can't believe this is happening. Having one of them to worry about is more than enough. Two is just awful."

Hunter brushed the flyaway hairs that had escaped her ponytail back and kissed her forehead. "Don't think about them anymore. I'm here, and neither of them will lay a hand on you."

She rested a hand on his chest, no doubt feeling the racing of his heart. "I'm okay. We need to be smart about this. I know you can't be with me all the time. I can defend myself. Really. I took self-defense classes after what happened with Dawn's old boyfriend."

Hunter rested his forehead against hers. "Why do all of her boyfriends come after you?"

"Because I wanted what was best for her. Which happened to not be them."

Hunter raised his head to study her face. What was best for Felicity? He wanted it to be him. She was selfless and kind, but all he had to offer her was his loyalty.

And his love. It was easy to give her that.

Pressure built in his chest, urging him to tell her that if she had nothing else in this world, she would always have him—all of him.

He opened his mouth to say as much when the laundry room door opened.

Though he and Felicity were wrapped up in each other, she didn't pull away or fumble to put distance between them when Micah barged in.

"Officer Guthrie is here. He wants to see you in the living room."

Great. A visit from any member of the police department besides Asa was never a good sign. "I'll be right there."

Micah left, closing the door behind him.

Felicity lifted her head, revealing the worry lines on her face. "What's that about?"

"I don't know. I'll come find you when I figure it out."

"Okay. I should be here a while. I need to get a few more loads folded before supper."

Hunter kissed her again before going to see what the police wanted with him this time.

Officer Guthrie stood near the fireplace when Hunter entered the living room. He'd expected to recognize the man, but he had no recollection of running into Officer Guthrie in Blackwater. His straight nose and lifted chin made him seem like the epitome of arrogance.

Hunter extended a hand. "Hunter Harding. How can I help you?"

Officer Guthrie accepted the hand and shook it with a strong grip. His intense stare made it clear he was to be respected as the law of the land, and the seeds of dislike sprouted in Hunter's mind. He reminded himself that looks could be deceiving and tried to give the guy a fair shake.

"There's been a police report filed regarding stolen lawn equipment from a local church. Since there was no sign of forced entry, our first suspects are those who hold keys to the building."

Typical. Something was stolen, and Hunter got the blame. Who in their right mind would steal from a church? "I guess that's me."

Camille stomped into the room wearing an unfamiliar scowl. "Don't say anything." She pointed at Hunter.

"This is a private conversation, ma'am," Officer Guthrie said with an air of entitlement that raked Hunter's nerves.

Camille's smile said she wouldn't be outmatched. "I'm his attorney."

Officer Guthrie inhaled and hooked his thumbs into his belt. Turning away from Camille as if he was annoyed by her presence, he said, "I have some questions for you."

Camille tapped on her phone. "Not yet. We have one more person joining us."

Officer Guthrie scowled but was smart enough to keep his mouth shut. Hunter was on the edge of telling the guy where he could take his holier-than-thou attitude when Haley walked in.

"Sorry, I was getting this." She handed a flash drive to the officer who accepted it with two fingers as if it were covered in slop.

"What is this?"

"It's the surveillance videos from the ranch from last night. Hunter was here. Also, I added the video from a few days ago that shows Hunter's dad sneaking into his cabin while we were in town."

Camille held up a finger. "For the record, the man's name is Butch Harding, and he's wanted for a dozen felonies and misdemeanors."

Officer Guthrie narrowed his eyes. "It's almost like you knew I was coming."

"We did," Haley said. "We just didn't know what the fallout would be for Butch sneaking around or what exactly he took."

"Sounds like it was the key to the church equipment building," Camille said with a winning smile.

"I didn't even mention what was stolen."

"You didn't have to. We knew Butch would steal something, and Hunter would be the suspect."

Camille's ire had reached a level Hunter had never experienced before, and he didn't want her to lose her cool fighting his battles for him, even if he did appreciate her legal services. "If you want to follow me to my cabin, I can show you where I keep the keys. I hadn't noticed they were gone, and I hadn't needed them yet. So if they aren't there, that's something you could put in your report."

"I'll come too. Just in case," Camille added.

Officer Guthrie bristled with annoyance. "Fine."

Hunter let Camille lead the way, and he was thankful Camille chose the back exit. The last thing he needed was for the guests to see him following an officer out the door.

It didn't take long to confirm the missing keys. Officer Guthrie wrote up his report and left in a worse mood than when he arrived.

When the door closed behind the officer, Camille turned on Hunter and growled, "I can't stand that guy."

"You know him?"

"Not really. I've had some legal interactions with him, and he thinks the enforcement side of the legal system trumps the others."

"I need to go find Felicity. I promised I would let her know what the guy wanted."

Camille tilted her head and sighed. "I love the two of you together. You're a perfect pair."

"You can take your mushy romance talk back to the main house with you."

"Oh, come on! Have you confessed your undying love to her yet?"

Hunter pointed at the door. "You're fired."

"Until next time," Camille said with a wave over her shoulder as she headed for the door.

A knock rattled the old wooden door as Camille's hand grasped the knob. "If that's Guthrie, I might kick him in the shin."

She opened the door before Hunter could discern her sincerity, but his worries faded when he saw Felicity carrying foil-covered plates. Boone and Dixie panted at her side.

"How did it go?" she asked anxiously.

Camille flipped her dark hair over one shoulder with a triumphant grin. "Fine. Officer Guthrie is a royal pain, but we had our evidence ready before he showed up."

"Evidence?"

Camille pointed over her shoulder. "I'll let Hunter explain. I need to run. I guess I won't see you two at supper?" she asked, eying the covered plates.

Felicity held them up. "I brought these in case Hunter didn't want to try to sneak back in without attracting attention."

As if he needed another reason to love Felicity. She understood him in ways he didn't even understand himself. "We won't be at supper."

"Bye," Camille sang as she headed for her car.

Hunter waved Felicity inside and took the plates from her. "Thanks for this."

"No problem."

"Let's eat, and I'll tell you about it," Hunter said as he unwrapped the food. He'd skipped lunch, and the hot meal smelled delicious.

Hunter had pieced together the reason for Officer Guthrie's visit by the time they'd finished eating.

"At least we know what Butch took now," she said as she pushed the remaining mashed potatoes around on her plate. "I can't believe he keeps taking from this place. They're his family. I get the impression that the Hardings are generous people."

"They are. Which makes what he did even worse. Everyone around here does their part, but Butch was always out for himself."

"Now he's working with Cain."

"Anything to make a buck," Hunter said. "Some things never change. He'd rather steal than do an honest day's work."

"And you'll be paying for his crimes."

Hunter tapped his knuckles on the hard wood of the table—the same table he'd sat at when he did his homework as a kid while his dad was out getting drunk and into trouble. "Some things never change."

Felicity covered his hand with hers, silencing the rapping of his knuckles and the thudding of his heart.

"Some things do change. That's what we're doing—breaking the cycle."

He turned his hand over and linked his fingers with hers, letting her skin and bones fill in the empty spaces. "You have anything going on tonight?"

"No. I finished up and rushed over here."

"There isn't much to do here. It's not like we can watch a movie or anything, but I'm not ready for you to leave."

Felicity's mischievous grin spread wide. "You could play."

Hunter glanced at the guitar in the corner. "Sure."

"And sing," she added.

He paused, but the usual rebuttal wasn't there. Instead, he *wanted* to sing for her, and peace settled over him. He didn't have a bad voice, but he'd never been comfortable sharing it.

She followed him to the living room where he picked up the guitar. He took a seat on the couch while she sat on the edge of the recliner, leaning forward, eager to hear the music.

He played a few chords before asking, "What do you want to hear?"

"Whatever you want to play."

Hunter slid the pad of his finger over a taut string as he considered his options. Then, he closed his eyes and thought about the song he wanted to sing. It was one he and Asher played often at Barn Sour, and he knew it well.

If he was going to sing for her, he might as well go for broke.

As he played the first chords of George Strait's "I Cross My Heart," Felicity propped her elbows on her knees and tucked her fist under her chin. Her attention stayed locked on him as he sang the song that best translated the way he felt about her.

And when she looked at him that way, he knew she was the one. The one who had already changed his life. The one who made him feel whole and appreciated.

When he finished the song and the lyrics were done, he wasn't sure what to say.

Thankfully, she spoke first. "Is this what you do every night? Sing to the walls?"

"Pretty much."

"I'm glad you sang for me," she whispered. "It was beautiful."

"You're changing everything about me."

She was. He'd done things with her that had never crossed his mind. She'd made him see the world in a different light and look for the good instead of the bad that followed him around.

She stood and stepped to the couch where she sat beside him. He moved the guitar from his lap and pulled her in close to his side.

Her head rested on his shoulder, easy and comfortable as if the two of them belonged here, wrapped up together.

"Don't sound so upset about it. You'll cut fewer people if you dull those sharp edges."

She was right. He'd been isolating himself for so long, opening his world to Felicity had been an unwelcome change at first. He had no idea how to be half of a whole. "I want to be good for you."

She lifted her chin and looked up at him. "You're doing just fine. Rocky start, but there's a learning curve."

Hunter swallowed hard and pushed the words that had lodged in his throat out into the air. "I love you."

Her gasp was quiet, and he took the opportunity her shock afforded him to dip his mouth to cover hers. He knew enough to know he'd put himself out on a ledge, and he might be standing alone. Not completely alone, but Felicity may not be beside him on the edge yet.

She turned her body toward him and rested her legs over his. He wrapped his arms tighter around her as her fingertips grazed over the scar on his face and trailed into his hair.

His grip on her hip tightened, and she pulled away in a rush before tucking her face between his shoulder and neck.

Desperate to calm his racing adrenaline, he removed his hands from her hip and back and sucked in a deep breath. He could control himself around her. Or at least he'd thought he could five minutes ago.

"I love you too."

Her murmured words were hard to make out, but he was sure he'd heard them.

She continued, and her shoulders straightened with her resolve. "You want to make all my dreams come true? I want you. You want to give me everything? I want you."

He felt it then—the shifting of the trajectory of his future. He'd been waking up each morning moving himself closer to death, but Felicity changed that.

Now, the only way to go was up.

Chapter Eighteen

FELICITY

Felicity had been so wrong about love. She'd prayed and doubted for years, but she would have never guessed Hunter would become the man she'd want to spend her life beside.

There were a dozen reasons why she hadn't seen it coming. She'd been distracted by one thing after the other. Her mother, her job, her cousin, everything else had seemed to require her full attention.

But with Hunter, she shared an unspoken understanding. He would lift her up, and she would stand bravely beside him.

She hadn't known what love would look like, but now she wondered how she didn't see it sooner. Hunter had always been here, and God had known his purpose in her life from the start. She'd been looking for something to fill the emptiness inside her—that hole her mother never filled with affection.

And that was where she'd been wrong. Love wasn't half for a half. It required two people willing to give their whole, brave selves to each other.

Felicity raised her head and looked into his eyes. "I love you."

She needed to say it again because the words felt bigger than one small sentence.

Hunter's phone rang, and he frowned. "I'm not answering questions about the police officer."

Felicity laughed and moved her legs from his lap. "Just see who it is."

He held up the phone for Felicity to see Haley's name on the screen.

Now it was Felicity's turn to frown. "She knows about the police. It must be something else."

Unhappy about the interruption, Hunter answered the call on speakerphone with a curt, "Hello."

"Is Felicity with you?"

He looked up at her and lamented the content look on her face from only moments ago. "Yes."

"Where are you?"

Haley used the rapid-fire question technique when she was worried, and Hunter tried to keep the muscles in his shoulders relaxed.

"My place."

Haley blurted out the reason for her call. "Butch and Cain are coming."

Hunter was on his feet and heading for the door. "Where?"

"They just crossed the property line. You have a few minutes, but it looks like they're heading for the cabins. I can't always see them."

He put the phone on the small, wooden table by the door while he slipped on a coat. It was navy and would blend in with the darkening night. "Felicity needs to get to the main house."

She was by his side in an instant. "I have to find Boone." Fear had her voice shaking as she grabbed Hunter's arm.

"Boone is with me," Haley assured.

"In the house?" Felicity asked.

"Yes. Just get over here," Haley demanded. "Hunter, Lucas is on his way. Laney is calling the others."

"What about Asa?" Hunter asked.

"Already on his way."

Hunter strode toward the only bedroom in the cabin, leaving the phone with Felicity.

"What can I do to help?" she asked.

"Nothing. The police will be here soon," Haley confirmed.

Hunter returned and pressed a pistol into Felicity's hand. "Do you know how to use this?"

She studied the gun and gauged her confidence in handling the weapon. It was heavier than she'd expected. "I think so." Her pulse thumped hard and hot in her ears. She'd never used a gun before, aside from some safety classes she'd taken years ago.

Hunter put both of his hands on her face and directed her attention to him. "This one is easy. Point and shoot."

She nodded, unable to speak assurances when she felt so unsure of everything.

"Hunter?" Haley's voice drew their attention to the phone beside them.

"Yeah?"

"Don't do anything you'll regret. Leave it to the police."

Felicity felt the restrained torque in his arms. "You're not going out there, are you?"

He didn't answer her. Instead, he picked up the phone. "I've got this."

"Really, just bring Felicity here, and we can all stay away from them while the police do their job," Haley reasoned.

"If they're out there, they're not leaving without a greeting from me," Hunter said.

Felicity tightened her grip on his arm. "No. Let's go to the main house."

Hunter opened the front door. "You go to the main house with Lucas, and I'll make sure they don't get too close to the cabins before the police get here."

The headlights of Lucas's truck lit up the front of Hunter's cabin, and he jerked his head toward the approaching vehicle. "Let's go."

"Guys," Haley said in a shaky voice. "They have to be getting close. Please leave."

Hunter put a hand on Felicity's back and herded her out the door. "Let's go."

"Come with me," she begged.

"I'll be right there," Hunter promised as he opened the passenger's side door of the truck. With a determined glance, he stilled Lucas from getting out of the truck. "Take her to the main house."

She slipped in, and Hunter leaned in to kiss her hard and fast.

"Please come with me," she said.

"You have to go."

"I'll be right back," Lucas promised Hunter.

A sinking feeling swirled in her gut as Hunter closed the door. She knew Cain wanted to get back at her for the fallout she'd caused with the fighting dogs, but she hadn't regretted any of it until now when Hunter might be in danger trying to protect her and the ranch.

Every inch of her skin prickled and crawled. It felt wrong leaving him. He could take care of himself, but she wanted to help. Her mind was spinning. How long would it take the police to get here? Would Butch and Cain make it to the cabins before help arrived?

Lucas shifted into gear and turned the truck toward the main house. They rode in silence for a moment before Lucas assured, "Hunter can handle it."

She tossed around the thoughts in her head, searching for a way to help. When Lucas parked at the main house, she rested a hand on his arm to stop him from getting out. "What if they get away?"

"I hope that doesn't happen," Lucas said.

"I have an idea. We can find where they parked and make sure they can't leave."

When Lucas didn't immediately reject the idea, she knew she was on to something.

"What kind of tools do you have?" she asked.

"Anything." He rubbed his hands over his face. "Hunter will kill me if I take you out there."

"Hunter gave me a pistol. Besides, Butch and Cain aren't there. They're headed for the cabins."

Lucas inhaled, and shifted into reverse. "We need to be quick." He turned the truck and headed for the ranch exit. She made a quick call to Camille who answered immediately.

"Hey, is everything okay?" Camille was no doubt helping Haley keep track of the surveillance footage.

"Yes, is there any surveillance around the road? Can you figure out where Butch and Cain parked?"

Camille whispered the question to Haley, and Felicity tapped her heel against the floorboard of Lucas's truck as she waited.

"I don't see a vehicle. There are only a few places I can see," Haley confirmed.

"Thanks."

"Wait. What are you doing?" Camille asked quickly. "Is Lucas with you?"

"Yes. We're going to make sure they don't get away."

"Asa said they're about five minutes out," Camille said. "Don't do anything crazy."

"Hunter gave me a gun," Felicity said. "Stay on the phone with me until we get there."

"Hunter is going to lose his mind if you don't get your behind to this house," Camille lectured.

"He'll also thank me if they try to make a run for it."

Camille huffed. "As your attorney, I have to advise you against this."

"That's much appreciated."

Lucas turned onto the main road and leaned into the accelerator. "We're almost there. This won't take long."

Lucas pulled the truck off the side of the road when they spotted Cain's burgundy truck parked just inside the tree line. It was the same vehicle she'd chased down the street after he'd taken Boone.

The sight of Cain's truck in the dim moonlight lit a fire in Felicity's resolve. He wouldn't take anything else from her, and she'd make sure of it.

"I think we should cut his battery cable. He won't be able to leave, and the police will have time to make it here before he figures it out."

"Put the phone in your pocket, but don't disconnect in case you need us," Haley said.

"Are you still on the phone with Hunter?" Felicity asked.

"No, we got cut off, but we're watching to see if anything happens. We can't see them right now."

Adrenaline pulsed through her veins. She wanted to be with Hunter somewhere far away from Cain and Butch. Instead, their enemies had separated them. She hoped this wasn't all a trap.

She shoved the phone in her pocket and jumped out of the truck. Lucas quickly searched the toolbox in the bed of his truck and came up with bolt cutters.

The tall grass in the ditch brushed against her jeans. It was so thick she had to high-step and pray there wasn't a snake hiding in the weeds.

"I'll disconnect it, and you call Asa," Lucas said. "Tell him where we are and to send someone here in case they try to make a run for it. We can have someone waiting at both places."

She pulled out her phone. "Guys, I have to call Asa."

"Hurry," Camille ordered. "We'll call you back if there's trouble."

Felicity made the call to Asa and waited what felt like forever for him to answer.

"Officer Scott."

"Asa, where are you?"

"Two minutes out."

"Cain's truck is parked off the road west of the ranch entrance. Can you send someone here?"

"Let me figure out how we can split this up."

Felicity's phone vibrated against her face, alerting her to another incoming call as Lucas lifted the hood of the truck. The scrape of rusted metal on metal screeched into the night, and she scanned the darkness around her.

"Caleb and Jennifer will be coming from that direction. I'll send them to meet you."

"Thanks. I have to go."

Lucas had just cut through the cable when thick arms grabbed him from behind.

"Lucas!" Felicity screamed as he flew backward.

After blindsiding Lucas and slamming him to the ground, Cain pinned him down with a leg on both sides and his body positioned above Lucas.

It was a memory, but it wasn't. Felicity had once been the one pinned down while her attacker dealt blow after blow to her face.

There was a moment of paralysis where her mind and body were at war.

And then she remembered what Hunter had done for Lucas and why he'd done it. If Hunter's bravery had taught her anything, it was that being selfless for others was worth the cost.

Cain had his back turned to her, and she only needed to distract him long enough for Lucas to get his bearings.

She lined up with Cain's side and crouched low. Pushing with all the power she had in her legs, she ran toward Cain and tackled him as best she could.

Unfortunately, her small weight had nothing on Cain, and she was only successful in knocking him off-balance. It didn't matter if she took him to the ground. Lucas just needed a chance to get the upper hand.

But before she could scramble away from Cain, his thick arms wrapped around her and picked her up, knocking her feet from beneath her, and slammed her into the ground.

Her head and right side hit first, and the impact knocked the breath from her lungs. The panic was instant when she couldn't catch her breath, and she couldn't even focus to drag herself out of Cain's reach.

Before she had a chance to attempt an escape, he was pinning her to the ground. The rage in his voice as he cursed her echoed in the quiet woods nearby. Her vision was blurry as Cain rose atop her like a tsunami ready to crash into the shore.

Suddenly, Cain disappeared, and she wasn't sure if she'd blacked out or if she'd only lost her vision, but the only thing she could see was black.

She could hear screams, so she hadn't lost consciousness. She felt as if her limbs were restrained to the ground. When she tried to move them, they just felt heavy.

She had to get up and help Lucas. She knew if Cain came back for her before she got her bearings, she'd die here on the side of the road.

It took her a moment to realize what she was hearing. It was a siren, and flashes of color pulsed through the blackness as her vision cleared.

Asa. It was Asa or someone else who could help them.

Lucas hurried to her, examining her from head to toe and supporting her with a firm hand on both shoulders. "Are you okay?"

"Yeah." It was the only word she could produce right now.

Lucas helped her to her feet and wrapped her in a hug. His chest heaved against her. "Don't scare me like that, woman."

"Cain?" she asked.

Lucas didn't answer, and she saw Micah running toward them, lit up in the blues of the police lights.

She sniffed, afraid to give in and let the tears come yet. But the ashy smell of smoke filled her senses, and she tensed.

Micah stopped at their side, and Lucas lifted his head at the same time Felicity did. An orange glow was just visible over the trees.

"Are you okay?" Micah asked as he gave Felicity a once-over.

She nodded, but her attention was fixated on the glow in the dark sky. Not the ranch. Not Blackwater. Not her home.

Police surrounded them, and she noticed Cain lying in the tall grass.

"Is he—"

"No. I don't think so," Lucas interrupted. "I hit him with the bolt cutters, but I don't think it was enough to kill him."

She stepped away from Lucas and covered her mouth and nose with her hands. The smell of smoke was getting stronger, and a new siren pierced the night along with the red flashes of a fire engine.

A few officers had made their way to check on Cain, and others were approaching.

The first officer she met was a young man, and the other was a dark-haired woman.

"What's happening over there?" Felicity asked, pointing to the orange clouds lifting over the ranch.

But she knew what it was, and she didn't want to hear the answer. She wanted to find her family and make sure they were okay. That was the only thing that mattered. She'd just found them, and she didn't want to lose them.

Chapter Nineteen

HUNTER

Hunter watched Lucas's headlights as he drove for the main house. As long as Felicity was safe, everything else would work out.

Right now, it was his mission to make sure Butch and Cain got a ride in a cop car.

Hunter's dad might be blood, but enough was enough. After the beatings he endured as a kid and having to see the aftermath when his dad took everything from the ranch, he wasn't about to let Butch take anything else.

Hunter had pocketed a gun for himself as well, but he didn't intend to use it unless he had no other choice. He might be out for justice tonight, but he didn't want to be the enforcer.

Haley had disconnected their call, but she was still texting him updates.

Haley: They're close. Please get out of there.

Haley: Asa is almost here. Let the police handle it.

Hunter intended to do just that. If possible, he'd just keep an eye on Butch and Cain and make sure they were apprehended. If needed, he'd take matters into his own hands.

With his back against the exterior of his cabin, he waited just around the corner and watched for Butch and Cain to step out of the woods behind the wranglers' cabins.

Taking money was one thing, but Butch probably knew good and well he wouldn't find any cash in the cabins. His cousins and their wives weren't sitting on a big bank roll or hiding it in a coffee can. Butch should know that, so why was he here?

Hunter heard them before he saw them. The crackling sound of their steps gave Hunter an idea of where they were, but seeing in the dark was impossible. He narrowed his eyes and focused on the line where the shadows of the trees ended and the moonlight dimly lit the clearing.

Hunter caught sight of Butch first, then Cain joined him as they headed toward the cabins. They walked with heavy footfalls, confident and bold, toward Hunter and Felicity's cabins.

It didn't make sense. Hunter didn't care for material possessions—never had. And he gave half of everything given to him to Silas and Anita, while another ten percent went to the church. There was little left, but he kept his meager savings in the bank, knowing his dad could sniff out cash a mile away.

Cain would be after Felicity's cabin, thinking he might find Boone nearby, but how did they know which cabin was hers?

Cain lifted his hands and looked at something he held, or was he toying with it? Hunter couldn't tell what it was in the dim light.

An orange spark flared, and Hunter's pulse raced. There had been a massive fire on the ranch when he was young, and he still remembered the fallout. The barns and main house were insured, but the cabins weren't. They might be a century old, but they were his family's homes.

For the first time, Hunter realized Butch probably started those fires. He'd always had an urge to destroy.

The kindling glowed brighter, and Hunter could make out the crude outline of a wad of burning paper.

He couldn't wait for Asa. Butch and Cain would have the cabins and forest on fire in minutes.

Hunter frantically kicked the heel of his boot into the dirt at his feet, stomping away the rocks and grass. When the dirt was exposed, he scooped up the largest handful he could and ran around the corner of the house.

He couldn't tell if Butch was surprised to see him or if he even recognized his own son. As soon as Hunter was close enough, he threw the dirt at the fire, knowing full well that the lines were drawn two against one.

Cain kept a tight hold on it, but the small flame was only weakened, not extinguished.

Butch barreled into Hunter's back, wrapping him in a tight hold. Hunter threw his head back, slamming it into Butch's nose.

Hunter had a few seconds to get his bearings before Butch was coming after him again. Cain hadn't joined the fight yet, and Hunter didn't know if that was a good sign or a bad one. Right now, he was thankful to only be matched against one.

Hunter and Butch fell to the ground, scuffling and grabbing. It wasn't lost on Hunter that their time was limited. He had no idea how much time he had, and Butch was fighting back with all he had.

On his knees behind Butch, Hunter hooked his arm around his dad's neck. He looked over his shoulder and caught sight of Cain, stoking the growing flames around the foundation of Felicity's cabin.

Hunter needed to stop Cain and put out the fire, but he couldn't release his hold on Butch.

Butch reached over his head, arms flailing and grabbing. "Get off!"

Butch had the seasoned strength of an older man, but Hunter had every advantage, and he'd been on guard for half of his life, waiting to protect this place and these people from his dad if necessary.

"You were always holding me back," Butch growled through his constricted throat, his words hoarse and forced.

Hunter tightened his grip around Butch's neck. He grabbed at Hunter's arm, clawing and pulling with everything he had.

Hunter heard the pounding of footsteps nearby and looked over his shoulder to see Cain running back into the woods with Micah and Noah on his trail.

Micah pointed at Felicity's burning cabin as he ran. "Noah."

Butch fought back with renewed energy when he saw Micah pursuing Cain.

Hunter held on tighter and seethed. Felicity had worked so hard to build a home here that she cared about, and once again the things she loved were being taken from her. "Was it worth it?" Hunter growled.

Butch mumbled something, trying to speak past the hold Hunter had on his throat. The few words that he would discern were "money" and "stupid dog."

"I protect my own, and you made a big mistake tonight," Hunter promised.

"Just let me go. I'll take the dog and leave."

"Not a chance. That's Felicity's cabin your friend set on fire!"

"He's just getting back at her."

"For what? She didn't do anything." Hunter panted as Butch continued to fight against his hold. "It's like a disease. You look like garbage."

"You were always in the way. I should'a gave you up when your mom left."

It didn't matter. Nothing Butch said mattered. All it did was fuel the fire in Hunter to hold out until the police arrived.

Time seemed to crawl as Hunter fought to maintain control over Butch. The longer they wrestled, the more Butch fought back. The old man had to tire out soon, but the promise of imprisonment was spurring his energy.

Finally, the flashing lights of the police strobed across the trees, and Butch fought back harder. Hunter knew he could hold his dad, but he hoped Micah had been able to catch up with Cain.

"Get off me!" Butch screamed.

Hunter held his ground. "Not a chance. You put my family in danger, and I'd do anything to keep them safe. I'm protecting my future like you never did."

Butch grunted and tried to force words out. "That girl!"

"She's my family! You don't get it." No, Butch had never understood love or loyalty. That's why he and Hunter had never been on the same side. Cruelty and greed could never know love.

Rapid footsteps approached behind Hunter. "Stop! Put your hands up!" an officer yelled behind him.

Hunter released Butch who quickly scrambled to his feet. He'd only made it a few steps toward the forest when two officers chased after him.

Hunter remained with his hands up as Asa joined him.

"They'll get him," Asa promised.

Hunter lowered his hands and panted. "Is Felicity okay? She should be at the main house."

"She called while I was on my way. She and Lucas were disabling Cain's vehicle."

"She what?" Hunter shouted. "Where is she?"

Asa rested a restraining hand on Hunter's shoulder and spoke into the radio on his shoulder. "Update on Cain."

A male voice responded. "Apprehended."

"Update on the female," Asa demanded.

"Safe," was the curt response.

Hunter released a tense breath. He wanted to say he couldn't believe she'd gone out there, but it wasn't a stretch to know she'd want to do something. She was strong, and she'd never been one to sit idle when she could help.

He looked behind Asa to the flames that engulfed one side of Felicity's cabin and lit the sky an ugly, hazy orange. The firefighters doused the dying flames, but there was still plenty of exterior damage.

Police and firefighters milled around the cabins and in the woods, taking care of the fire and getting Butch into a police vehicle. Hunter didn't give the man a second glance. He had more important things to worry about.

Asa was talking to another officer, and Hunter got his attention. "I have to go find Felicity. Where did she say they were?"

"Hunter!"

He recognized the voice before he saw her. Felicity ran straight for him and into his arms.

Feeling the weight and reality of Felicity wrapped around him was a balm to his tired soul. Hearing her and seeing that she was all right was the only thing he needed right now.

The smell of smoke filled his senses, but Felicity was the only thing that mattered. This was the reason he'd turn on his flesh and blood. This was the reason he knew right from wrong. This was why he'd risk everything for her.

Chapter Twenty

FELICITY

Felicity clung to Hunter. With her arms wrapped around him, it was as if the world around them blurred. She squeezed her eyes closed and buried her nose in the rough material of his jacket, blocking out the scene around them.

She didn't want to see the charred wall of her cabin. She didn't want to smell the burning wood. She didn't want to hear the crackling and roaring of the dying flames.

That cabin was the home she'd always wanted. It was a shelter from the pain of the past—a place surrounded by people she loved. It was a reminder that her past was a lesson, not a life sentence. She'd been free to overcome the hurt and move on here. She could learn to forgive without the closure of apologies because she was growing into a better person.

"I love you," Hunter whispered as he stroked a gentle hand over her hair.

She'd lost everything, but Hunter was still standing beside her. She was breaking, but it wasn't a cruel disturbance. She was breaking like the dawn: a beautiful beginning. Her new life was going to cost her the old one, but she didn't mind.

This was her shelter. Hunter was her home. They were leading each other out of the darkness.

The clearing behind the cabins was bustling with first responders, but the only thing she could hear was the beating of Hunter's heart against her ear.

Asa approached, and she lifted her head from Hunter's chest. "Thank you."

"I don't want to give false hope, but I think this is a huge win for all of us. We have a growing list of charges for both of these men, and I think this might be enough to prove the danger they pose to society."

Hunter scoffed. "Could they be called anything else?"

"The justice system is a slippery slope, but they'll be out of my hands soon."

"Can I go check on Boone?" Felicity asked.

"Of course," Asa said. "I'll call you with any questions."

Hunter extended a hand to his friend. "I appreciate what you did."

Asa grasped the hand tightly. "Don't mention it."

Hunter kept his arm around her shoulders as they walked around the cabins, giving hers a wide berth so the firefighters could do their job. There wasn't a single thing inside the structure she needed. Her everyday things were at Asher and Haley's, but she didn't own anything she would grieve for after this.

When they walked around Hunter's cabin, they caught sight of Lucas at the same moment he saw them and came running over.

"Hey, everything okay?" Lucas asked.

"I think so," Hunter said with hesitation in his tone. "Did I hear you took Felicity to disable the vehicle?"

Lucas took a tentative step back and tucked his shoulders in. "Maybe."

Felicity laid a hand on Hunter's chest. "We did it, and neither of us were hurt."

"I can't say the same for Cain," Lucas added.

"What happened to him?" Hunter asked.

Lucas straightened his shoulders. "I may have knocked him out with the bolt cutters."

Hunter huffed. "He had it coming."

"Just keeping the wolves away," Lucas said.

Felicity and Lucas had taken a huge risk tampering with Cain's vehicle, but it had been necessary. If they hadn't hindered him, Cain would have been long gone by the time the police arrived.

"Thanks." There was reverence and appreciation in Hunter's voice. The sacrifice of Hunter's childhood had come full-circle.

"We're still not even," Lucas said.

"I saved your life, and you saved mine. Sounds like we are."

Lucas patted Felicity on the shoulder. "You did a great job out there."

"Thanks again," Felicity said. "We're headed to the main house. I'll let Maddie know you're okay."

"I'd appreciate that." Lucas made a gesture of tipping his hat and went to join his brothers.

Hunter led Felicity to his truck and opened the passenger side door for her before walking around and taking his own place behind the wheel. He held her hand as they drove to the main house.

When Hunter parked the truck, he lifted the hand holding hers and pulled her closer. His lips met hers in a rush that stole her breath, capturing her heart in the safe shelter of his arms.

He pulled back slightly and cradled her cheeks in his hands. "I want to hear about what happened out there, but not tonight."

"Same. I'm exhausted."

He kissed her once on the forehead before getting out of the truck. She met him at the base of the small stairs leading up to the porch, and they went inside together.

The lights of the main house were blindingly bright, and half a dozen people stood from where they'd been sitting at the long table. Chairs scraped the floor as everyone began talking at once, asking questions and exclaiming their thankfulness.

Haley was on the opposite side of the large meeting room, but she broke into a run when she spotted Hunter and Felicity.

Haley barreled into Felicity, embracing her so tightly, the sobs broke from both of them.

She'd had a rocky, life-long bond with Dawn, but this connection with Haley and the other women at the ranch was stronger than anything Felicity had ever known. It was the power of courage and acceptance. It was pure and selfless like nothing she'd known before she came to Blackwater.

"Thank you," Felicity whispered.

"Don't ever scare me like that again," Haley demanded.

Boone's bark rose above the voices, and he brushed against Felicity's leg, demanding attention.

Felicity bent to him, but the tears began anew as she hugged her friend. Cain had taken so much from her, but if she focused on the things she still had, it felt as if she had it all.

"Felicity!"

She looked around for Jameson and saw him pushing his way through the Harding family to get to her.

"What happened?" he asked, unbelieving of the chaos going on over the hill.

She couldn't tell him yet. She didn't have the words to speak. Instead, she wrapped her arms around him, and as he held her, she prayed. Prayed for peace, understanding, and guidance.

Felicity looked up at Jameson and wiped the tears from her eyes. "I'm okay. I'm great."

"You're great? I'm getting a call that Cain Jenkins *and* Butch Harding are here, and you're great!"

"Okay, I'm not great, but I am fine."

"We'll get you set up in a different cabin, and it'll be better than the other one," Haley promised.

Felicity looked for Hunter. Sure, she wanted to still live here on the ranch, but she'd loved living beside Hunter. They'd formed a silent routine, even if she'd been sleeping at Asher and Haley's place lately.

Hunter was there, waiting patiently beside her, as he always would. The man was sturdier than an oak tree, and as unyielding as the mountains.

"You obviously need to get checked out. Did Noah check your vitals?" Jameson asked.

Felicity had to laugh. There was humor in her brother's overreaction, and she was grateful she had family left who cared.

Mama Harding laid a comforting hand on Felicity's shoulder. The older woman was like the mother she'd only read about in stories. She'd thought it was all fiction and fantasy. She'd truly believed families were dysfunctional, until Silas and Anita showed her what supportive and loving parents looked like.

"You need some rest," Mama Harding said.

"Come on. The police and the firefighters have everything handled. Let's get you to bed," Hunter said.

Exhaustion hit Felicity like a brick at the mention of rest. She'd been so worried throughout the night that she'd been running on adrenaline for hours now.

Asher slapped a hand on Hunter's shoulder. "Let's go get you some clothes. Your place will smell for a while, so you can take the other bedroom at our place."

Hunter looked at Felicity, and her heart soared. She didn't want to be far from him tonight. She'd sleep better knowing he was in the next room.

He grabbed her hand and squeezed. "Let's go."

***

The next morning, Felicity studied the charred remains of the small cabin where she'd lived for the last few months. What had made this place a home? How could she recreate that safety in the new cabin the Hardings had assigned to her?

"It's Noah's old place. You'll like it," Camille said as she slid the pendant of her necklace back and forth across the chain.

"I will. I don't know if I can salvage anything. The smell is so bad." Felicity pulled the collar of her shirt over her mouth and nose.

Noah rested a hand on the small of Camille's back. "You shouldn't be out here."

"I know. I'm leaving." Camille rubbed her hand up and down Felicity's upper arm. "I just wanted to see if you needed anything."

"I'm fine. Really. Thanks for everything."

"I'm only a call away."

Felicity waved good-bye to Camille. When she looked back at the cabin, she remembered the first time Hunter had kissed her on the porch.

"What's got you smiling?" Hunter asked.

"You."

She'd have to rebuild her life, but a beginning follows an ending. The next chapter of her life was a clean slate, but it had good bones. There was a man who would build it with her from the ground up, and there was a group of people who would be there with them through it all.

She didn't feel homeless. She felt full—full of everything that mattered.

Her Father in heaven had looked down and seen her in ruins. He lifted her up, carried her here, and put these friends in her path to change her fate.

Hunter wrapped an arm around her shoulder, but she turned and faced him, resting her arms on his shoulders and around his neck. Looking up into his emerald eyes, she could see the future, and it was beautiful.

"I'm fine. This should be devastating to me, but it isn't. I don't feel broken. I feel…" She squinted as she searched for the right word. "I feel new. I'm ready to get started on something bigger and better. All the bad parts of my life are gone."

She gripped Hunter's face. "I'm happy. I should be sad and alone, but I'm not." She was so full of love and hope that the darkness couldn't touch her. During the most trying night of her life, Hunter had fought for her, with her, and beside her for their shared future.

Hunter pressed his lips to hers, and a content moan emanated from her chest. He lifted her off her feet and squeezed her body tight against his.

There would always be a big, huge past behind her, but that's where it would stay. She was made for bigger and better things. The past didn't exist in the face of the things to come.

Chapter Twenty-One

HUNTER

Hunter had moved back into his cabin the week after the fire. It had taken a while to get the smell of smoke out, but Jade and Laney had worked hard to wash everything from ceiling to floor in every cabin.

A month after the fire, Felicity was settled into her new place. She'd moved in and quickly made the place her own.

Hunter stepped onto her porch after a long summer workday and felt the relief of the day's end wash over him. A wide-mouthed pot sat on a metal stand beside her door. The delicate white flowers had yellow centers. Felicity called them her happy reminders. Flowers sometimes bloomed in even the worst environments, and she'd done the same.

The summer sun was just beginning its descent in the sky. He liked the longer days this time of year, but it made it harder to sneak over to Felicity's place in the evenings without everyone and their mother seeing him.

Some things never changed. He'd never get used to attracting attention—good or bad.

He knocked on her door and waited.

Felicity yelled from within, "Come in!"

Inside, Felicity was putting an old receipt in a book she was reading. "You don't have to knock."

Hunter bent down to kiss her on the forehead. "Just let me do it."

She huffed and rested back in the recliner. "Fine."

He grinned. Her irritation at his knocking was reasonable. He'd been politely requesting entrance into her home, her heart, and her life for months. Every time, her door was always opened to him.

It wasn't so much a test as something he considered a novelty. If he had his way, they'd both be walking in the same front door every night.

Hunter pointed to the devotional she'd laid on the end table. "What's the lesson this week?"

The women had started up a weekly meeting, and the most Hunter could get out of them was that they had a discussion topic. Whatever they did, it was working for Felicity. He could see the light in her eyes when she talked about getting together with the girls.

"Contentment," she said with a grin. "Something I'm learning."

He hoped she was content. She smiled a lot, and she made a point to kiss him every time they saw each other. She'd lay one on him in front of the family, guests, or the church members, and she didn't care who saw. Hence his continued struggle with attracting attention.

But every time she singled him out of a crowd and dropped everything to run into his arms, he didn't care who was watching. He was a blessed man to have Felicity at his side.

His phone vibrated in his pocket. He didn't move to answer it, and he hoped Felicity hadn't heard it. He wasn't about to let anything steal his time with her.

Felicity stared at him, clearly waiting for him to answer.

"I don't want to talk to anybody," he said.

Felicity tilted her head and grinned. The look was confident and reprimanding at the same time, and Hunter knew what she wanted.

He huffed and pulled the phone from his pocket. "Hello."

"I'm sorry to call you after you've already headed home for the night, but could you come to the main house?" Mama Harding asked.

"Sure. I'll bring Felicity too." If Mama Harding needed help, they could get the job done faster with more helping hands.

"No, just you, please," Mama Harding requested.

Asking questions would only delay further. "I'll be right there."

He disconnected the call and rested his head back against the couch. "Mama Harding wants me at the main house."

Felicity stood. "I'll come with you."

"Actually, she said not to bring you."

Felicity's smile withered. "Why?"

He shrugged. "Beats me, but I'll let you know what it's about." He stood and pressed a hard kiss to her lips before heading for the door. "Love you."

"Love you too," she answered.

It was hard to be irritated with Mama Harding when she asked so little of him. Especially after all she'd done for him.

The main house was beginning to quiet down after supper. His cousins and their wives had mostly gone, and the guests had retired to their rooms or the rocking chairs on the front porch of the main house. Laney and Jade were cleaning the tables, and each gave him a soft, "Hey," as he walked through the meeting room to the kitchen.

Asher and Haley stood at the sink washing and drying dishes.

Haley jerked her head toward the door. "Silas and Mama Harding said they're waiting for you in the living room."

"Is anyone else in there?" Hunter asked.

"Nope. They just said they wanted to talk to you."

He was starting to feel singled out. "Thanks." It was probably something about Butch's sentencing. Hunter had tried to forget about his dad's upcoming trial, but the nagging worry that Butch would be allowed to sneak back into their lives to destroy again kept him up at night. There were too many people here he needed to protect from that evil.

In the living room, his aunt and uncle sat relaxed on the couch, but they stood when Hunter entered.

Silas's green eyes that mirrored Hunter's own were encircled by lines and wrinkles from his lifted cheeks. Anita wore the same joyful expression as every day, except it was moderately brighter.

"Have a seat, son," Silas said, pointing to the empty recliner.

Hunter sat and rubbed his sweaty palms over his jeans. "Is everything okay?"

"Of course," Anita promised. Her smile stretched farther than usual. "We have something for you."

Silas produced a folded piece of paper from his shirt pocket and handed it to Hunter.

Resting his elbows on his knees, Hunter opened the paper. His name was written in Silas's shaky handwriting above a number that had as many zeros as his truck had wheels.

"What's this?" Hunter tried to hand the check back to Silas. "This isn't mine."

Anita held up a hand, pushing the check back toward Hunter. "Yes, it is."

"We know it's you that sends the money with Asa every month," Silas said.

Hunter tensed. "How did you know?"

Anita chuckled. "We know you. You've been carrying the burden for what Butch did your whole life, and it's time you stopped that."

Hunter still held out the check. "I didn't give it to you to get it back."

Silas leaned forward and rested his elbows on his knees, calm and sure as always. "We always intended to give the money back to you."

"We were just holding it for you," Anita said.

Silas nodded to the check. "Life has a funny way of keeping score, and you've been winning all along." He tilted his head and scrunched his lips to one side. "This isn't actually your money."

"We've given each of our kids a starter fund. We don't want you to worry about money when you're starting a family."

Hunter huffed and stared at a darkened spot on the wooden floor. "I'm not your son."

"Oh, don't give us that," Anita reprimanded. "You're ours as much as any of the others."

"I'm not starting a family," Hunter argued.

Anita's eyes widened. "Look me in the eye and tell me you haven't thought about proposing to Felicity, and I still won't believe you."

Hunter tucked his chin and covered his face. He hadn't been quiet about his feelings for Felicity in weeks.

Anita leaned over to rest a hand on Hunter's shoulder. "We have a feeling you and Felicity won't be having a fancy wedding, but this combined with the rest that we've been hanging onto for you could get you a running start on a nice home for the two of you."

Hunter raised his head. "You want us to move?" He couldn't keep the shock from his tone.

He didn't want to leave the ranch, and neither did Felicity.

"No," Silas said. "We'd always planned to deed a piece of land to you, just like our other boys and their wives. Noah and Camille got the first pick. I guess we always knew they'd marry quickly once they got their feelings sorted out."

"Then Asher and Haley were ready to start a family from the get-go. So, they got the second pick," Anita explained.

Silas rubbed his chin. "Aaron and Jade have a place picked out. They need a bigger home since they already have Levi, and hopefully more children soon."

Anita looked to her husband for assurance before continuing. "We talked to our financial advisor, and we'll be giving you a hefty check four times a year until it's all paid back to you."

Hunter rubbed the pad of his thumb over the edge of the check. From the rough math he could do in his head, he'd given his aunt and uncle enough money to pay for a decent size house to be built.

The thought of having a real house here had never crossed his mind. Marriage hadn't crossed his mind either, until Felicity crashed into his life. Now, he was the guy with a ring picked out in the next town.

"I wanted you to have it. I can't pay you back for all you did for me—"

"Stop right there," Anita said with a hand in the air. "You don't owe us anything, just like our kids don't owe us anything."

Hunter pushed his hands through his hair. "What will Felicity think about all this?"

"She won't think anything different," Anita said. "She knows you're a good man, and you have a lot to offer her. Not a house or a ring, but a life of happiness and love. She already loves you just as you are, and I bet she'd be happy to live in one of the old wranglers' cabins with you. But it'd do you some good to get out of that place. You need a new place without memories of Butch."

"I want to give her all those things," Hunter said.

Silas tilted his head toward the check Hunter held. "This is the start of something new for both of you."

Hunter stood and held out a hand to Silas. "Thank you."

Silas accepted the hand but pulled Hunter in and embraced him.

His uncle's words were quiet beside Hunter's ear. "I'm proud of you."

Silas released him, and Anita opened her arms. Tears wet her lashes, and she bit her lips between her teeth to contain her smile. Hunter leaned down to hug his aunt. She may be smaller, but she was as strong as any man on this ranch. She and Silas had created a legacy that would resonate through the small town for years to come.

When Hunter released her, he looked from his aunt to his uncle. "Can I have the morning off? There's something I need to do in Bryson City."

Anita smiled. "Take the day. We can't wait to welcome Felicity to the family."

The family. His family would become her family, and they would have more people in their daily support system than they knew what to do with.

Hunter knew all the ways his dad had messed up, but knowing what not to do wasn't the same as knowing how to do things right.

Anita brushed her hand over the scar on Hunter's cheek. "You're going to make a wonderful husband for that woman."

He wasn't sure how she'd known what he was thinking, but Mama Harding's assurance was exactly what he'd needed to hear.

He may not have all the answers, but he'd spend the rest of his life figuring things out with Felicity by his side.

Epilogue

CAMILLE

Camille took deep breaths and fanned her hand in front of her face. Sweat dripped down the back of her neck and beaded on her temples.

"Wyoming has never been this hot before. Why now?" she asked.

Noah stepped into the garage where Camille waited. "It's not hotter than normal, but your hormones are probably to blame."

"What's that supposed to mean?" Camille snapped.

Noah kissed her forehead. "Nothing bad. It's probably normal for women eight months pregnant, no matter what season."

Camille propped her hand on her back and inhaled the deepest breath she could. "My ribs are crowded. Everything is crowded. My lungs can't even expand to get a full breath."

"We should just stay home. You need to rest and put your feet up."

"No, no. I'm just complaining. I'm not missing the reception." Camille jolted. "Oh, I forgot the present!"

Noah made to stop her. "Tell me where it is, and I'll get it."

Camille waved a hand. "I don't really know. I put it somewhere in our room."

"We'll find it," Noah assured as he guided Camille back up the three stairs leading into the house.

Camille stood in the center of their bedroom and scanned the surfaces. Had she put it in the closet? Did she shove it under the bed? The dresser drawer? She cupped her cheeks and searched her memory. Since the accident where she'd lost so many of her memories, she'd spent many hours in frustration searching for things and pieces of the past that had been lost to her. If she couldn't remember where she put the gift, the others would be upset. They'd worked so hard to find Felicity the perfect gift.

Tears welled in Camille's eyes, and Noah put his hands on her shoulders. "Don't worry. We'll find it. Even if we don't find it today, you can give it to her when it shows up."

Camille shook her head and bit her lip, forcing the tears to retreat. "I hate it when this happens."

Noah wrapped his arms around her, and she rested her head against his chest. She relaxed into his embrace and took a deep breath. This one actually felt satisfying, like breaking through the surface of the water after holding a breath for too long.

When her frantic worry had subsided, she raised her head and reached for her locket. Her eyes widened, and she hastily patted her collar. "My necklace." It was the one Noah had given her when they first started dating. She wore it every day. How had she forgotten it?

"I'll get it," Noah said as he stepped toward the nightstand. He pulled out the necklace and a small white bag with a pink bow. "Is this the gift?"

The weight on Camille's shoulders eased, and new tears pricked her eyes. "Yes!" She cupped her face in her hands and sobbed, thankful to have found Felicity's present.

Noah wrapped his arms around her again. "Hey, everything is fine. We found it."

"I know," Camille garbled. "I'm just so happy."

Her happiness was bigger than relief at finding the gift. She was grateful to have a husband who understood why it was important to find the things she misplaced. He knew how to comfort and calm her when she was frustrated with herself. He didn't leave her to tackle any problem alone. He never had. Even when they'd been friends, he'd been by her side every step of the way.

Now, she had a family that was growing in every direction. Camille had always been an only child, but now she had sisters, brothers, and nephews.

Soon, she'd have a son, and she thanked God every day for each blessing—old and new.

MADDIE

"Maddie!" Lucas yelled as he stepped into the stables.

"I'm coming. I'm coming," Maddie shouted over her shoulder before turning back to the filly nestled in the hay in front of her. She secured the bow loosely under the filly's neck. "I'll be back soon. Mama will take care of you while I'm gone."

Maddie stood and rubbed Goldie's mane. "You want a treat, Mama?" She handed the horse her favorite apple snack and rubbed the dirty hand off on her jeans.

Lucas's steps were quick as he sprinted through the stables looking for Maddie. "Seriously, I promised Haley we wouldn't be late." He stopped when he saw Maddie in Goldie's stable. "Have you had a shower?" he asked.

"Um, this morning," Maddie answered meekly. "I can clean up quickly."

Lucas extended his hand to her. "Come on."

She accepted it with a smile. "I had to make sure her present was ready."

"I'm not sure how much Felicity is going to like your gift," Lucas said. He was trying his best to let her down easy.

"She'll love it. You'll see."

"I'm not sure what I'll see, since Felicity has been here almost six months and hasn't been to the stables once."

"Ugh," Maddie grunted. "Your negativity is bringing me down."

Lucas stopped, and she almost crashed into him.

"What are you doing?" she asked.

"I'm growing up." Lucas looked at her with a bewildered expression. "Is this what it feels like to be a responsible adult?"

Maddie laughed and swatted his arm. "Get in the truck. You've still got some growing up to do."

"You ready to have kids?" he asked.

She looked up at her husband and wondered why he'd waited so long to bring it up. "I am."

Lucas nodded, and his expression was serious. "I am. I've been ready for a while, but I don't want to try unless you're ready."

Her chin began to quiver, so she wrapped her arms around his neck and buried her face in the crook of his neck. "I'm ready."

She'd been a child without parents, but she and Lucas were going to be the best parents when the Lord decided it was time. Lucas's heart was pure and full of love, and she couldn't be happier.

She released him and wiped the lone tear from her cheek. "Well, I guess it's settled."

"You want to—"

"Nope. We have a party to get to."

HALEY

Haley slapped a piece of tape over the end of the wrapping paper. "Not gonna be late. Not gonna be late," she mumbled to herself as she secured the rest of the wrapping.

She looked around the room, tapping a finger on her chin. "Where did I put that bow?"

Asher stepped into the room with the sparkly silver bow on his forehead. "Never fear, your hero is here!"

Haley chuckled and extended her hand. "Give me that."

"It'll cost you one kiss."

"I'd love to pay, but I can't get up," Haley said, gesturing to her large belly. Little Caleb would be here any day now, which left Haley feeling run down by the extra weight she carried.

Asher knelt beside her and handed over the bow.

Haley slapped the shimmery accessory on the present and opened her arms to Asher. "Thank you."

He held one hand and wrapped the other around her middle, hoisting her up with grunts and panting.

When Haley was on her feet, she sighed. "Whew. I think I need to sit down."

"Not on the floor," Asher joked.

"I don't think I'll be doing that again until after baby Caleb is born."

Asher took Haley's hands and led her to sit on the bed. "We don't have to go."

"Oh, yes we do! This is Felicity and Hunter. They're *married*. Did you hear what I said?"

"Hunter is married, and we're all surprised." Asher's attention was fixed on her hand where his thumb drew circles over the smooth skin. "They'll be good for each other."

Haley squeezed his hand. "I know. I'm just so happy for them."

"Maybe he'll start singing again. Felicity said he's got a great voice."

Haley brushed her fingers over her husband's cheek. She'd kept her voice bottled up when she'd first met him. She'd finally told him how she felt with a song, and her life had been better ever since. "He'll sing when he's ready."

Asher's hand cradled the back of her neck as he kissed her hard and sweet. Haley breathed in the moment, feeling revived by her husband's touch.

Hunter didn't need a voice. Maybe all he needed was a love like this—what he'd found with Felicity, and what they'd all found at Blackwater Ranch.

LANEY

"I have no idea what I'm doing," Laney whispered to the fancy candle stand she centered in the middle of the table.

"I don't think there's a wrong way," Micah said behind her.

Laney startled, almost knocking over the fancy centerpiece. "Good grief. Don't sneak up on me like that."

Micah wrapped his arms around her from behind and kissed her temple. "Relax. Hunter and Felicity don't care about this stuff."

"That's true, but I want it to look nice."

"It's just the family," Micah reminded her. "We don't have anyone to impress."

Laney turned in his arms and rested her hands on his chest. "I want them to have a good reception."

Micah looked around, studying the flowers and draped banners in the church fellowship hall. "It looks great."

Laney had put a lot of work into the decorations and food. With Mama Harding attending the ceremony, Camille and Haley in their third trimesters, Maddie making sure the new filly was doing well, and Jade wrangling Levi, Laney had put together the small reception for the family on her own.

Jameson jogged through the door wearing a nice pearl snap shirt and what they all called church boots. "It's over. They're taking pictures."

Laney waved a hand at him. "Shouldn't you be out there?"

"I already did that," Jameson assured.

"That must mean they're almost finished," Laney said. Excitement brewed in her middle as she waited to greet her new sister-in-law.

Truly, the women who married Micah's brothers felt more like family than her own. She'd somehow stumbled into marriage, friendships, and a welcoming family all at once.

Laney looked up at her husband, and the love in his expression flipped a switch. Her happy expression crumbled, and the sobs began instantly.

"Laney? Laney, what's wrong?" Micah held her and gently rocked from side to side.

She buried her face in his nice shirt, letting the fabric soak up the tears. "I think I'm pregnant."

"What?" Micah said, pulling her away from his chest to study her face. "What did you say?"

"I don't know, but there have been some signs." She twisted the material of his shirt sleeve in her fist, trying to anticipate his reaction.

"You don't know! Let's go find out!"

"Now?" Laney asked.

"Now." Micah grabbed her hand and pulled her toward the exit. "Jameson, you're in charge."

Jameson nodded, accepting his promotion with ease. "Got it, boss."

"Micah, wait." Laney pulled on his hand. "We can't just leave. The reception is about to start."

"We can run to the store and be right back. They won't even miss us," he promised.

Laney wiped the lingering tears from her face. "What if it's positive?"

Micah stopped his speedy walk through the church halls and turned to her. "It'll be great. We can tell everyone tomorrow."

"Slow down," Laney said with a shaky hand on his chest. "What if—"

Micah cradled her face in his hands and kissed her forehead before fixing his gaze on her. "Then we'll keep trying."

They'd only been "trying" for a few weeks, and they'd agreed to try their best not to be pressured or let expectations become a stressor, but all those things were easier said than done, especially when they were so ready to start a family.

"I love you," Laney whispered.

"I love you too. Now, let's go. I can't wait any longer."

Micah's excitement had the corners of her mouth turning up. She'd been blessed beyond measure, and she hoped they'd have more than one reason to celebrate this evening.

JADE

"Hop to it. We're going to be late," Jade said as she gently nudged Levi's back.

"We can count the cracks in the concrete on our way out," Aaron promised.

Levi huffed. "It'll be dark then, and I won't be able to see them."

"Can you count fast?" Jade asked.

Levi tucked his chin and picked up the pace.

Aaron draped his arm over Jade's shoulders. "How do you do that?"

"Do what?" she asked, a little dazed looking up at her husband. There were still times when he looked at her and stole her breath. Cleaned up for Hunter and Felicity's wedding reception, he was handsome enough to have her tripping over her own feet if she wasn't careful.

"How do you say simple things that are always the right thing?"

Jade scoffed. "Competition works every time, even if he's competing with himself."

Aaron looked over his shoulder to where Levi walked behind them. "That's a good thing. He's already smart as a whip. He'll be counting his way to a college degree before we know it."

Jade *did* trip over her feet at the imagery Aaron drew. "College?" she whispered.

"Yeah, hopefully one day."

She steadied herself and jerked her attention to Levi. He was only six. He couldn't go to college.

Aaron's hand rested on her hip. "Hey, I didn't mean to rattle you. We have a long time before he leaves us."

Levi's counting rose higher. "Thirty-seven. Thirty-eight."

"Jade, look at me," Aaron said as he leaned down to put his face closer to her level.

There was assurance in his eyes, but she'd just about fallen apart at the mention of college. Levi was still her little boy, and she was sure she'd always see him that way—learning and growing beside her and his dad.

"Don't worry about college."

Levi stepped up beside Jade and Aaron. Levi was still counting, but she reached for his little hand. He didn't miss a beat.

Aaron took her other hand, linking his fingers with hers. "I love you."

Her heart swelled. She had the love of a good man and a special boy. She'd be smart to hold onto these moments when they were both beside her.

"Felicity is gonna love my present," Levi said.

Jade swallowed the lump in her throat and nodded. "Yeah, she will."

He'd spent the last week painting a flower pot stand for Hunter and Felicity's front porch. Levi thought it was extra special because it could hold more than one flower.

Hearts were special that way, too. They could hold more than one love and bind to more than one heart. That was how she'd come to love a man and his son. Every beat of her heart was a promise that she would be bound to these two men forever.

FELICITY

"Open mine first!" Levi screamed and pointed to a massive blob with a sheet draped over it. "Sorry I couldn't wrap it, but it was just too big."

Felicity stood from the chair where she'd just settled to open the gifts from the family. She gathered the sides of her simple wedding dress into her fists. It wasn't one of those massive dresses that made a bride look like a cupcake. It was a simple white V-neck dress, but she couldn't keep her hands off the silky skirt.

She reached for the sheet, eager to find out what Levi had given them.

"Look over here!" Haley shouted, ready to snap a photo.

The muscles in Felicity's cheeks twitched. She'd never smiled so much in her life, but she couldn't stop it if she tried. Joy filled her, radiating from the inside out.

With Haley's approval, Felicity raised the sheet, revealing a metal stand with four platforms, each topped with a terracotta pot painted in different colors.

Felicity's vision blurred as she imagined the beautiful plants she could grow in these pots.

"Do you like it?" Levi asked.

Felicity nodded emphatically. The pristine curls Camille had crafted in Felicity's hair before the wedding tickled her neck with the movement. "I love it."

"You can put *four* different plants in that thing," Levi said.

Felicity laid a hand on his shoulder. "Will you help me decide which to plant?"

"Sure. I don't know their names, but I can just point out the ones I like best."

"Thanks. I love it," she said as she took her seat again. Hunter sat beside her, more than willing to let her open the gifts while he offered quiet thanks.

"Mine next!" Haley screamed with enough excitement to match Levi.

She shuffled over in her heels and laid a heavy rectangle present in Felicity's lap.

She looked to Hunter, silently questioning whether he wanted in on the gift unwrapping. His subtle nod toward the waiting gift was answer enough, and she ripped into the paper. With the wrapping laid open in her lap, Felicity gaped at a painted scene of a cabin—her old cabin—rendered on fresh wood.

"Did you paint this?" Felicity asked.

"I did. It wasn't hard to remember what your old place looked like. And I added Dixie and Boone," Haley said, pointing to the border collie and Black and Tan resting on the porch.

It was her first home here, the place that had tied her to the ranch and these people, and the house where she'd decided to open her heart.

"Look at the back," Haley prompted.

Felicity turned it over and read the verse that was beautifully written in black ink. "So now faith, hope, and love abide, these three; but the greatest of these is love. 1 Corinthians 13:13."

Faith, hope, and love had worked hand in hand to bring her here today. She stared at the words until Hunter's hand rested on hers.

She looked up at his ready expression. He'd be beside her through everything now—faith, hope, and love entwined into the bond they'd made tonight before their family and God.

Maddie cleared her throat. "My gift isn't here. Well, it's actually a gift from all of us. We'd like for you to name the new filly."

Felicity's eyes widened. "Really? Me?"

She turned to Hunter, but he held up both hands in surrender. "No, they said you."

"But I haven't seen it," she said.

Maddie toyed with the end of her braid. "I can take you to see it when we leave here. If you want," she added.

Felicity thought a moment before answering. "I'd like that."

Jameson stood and handed a box to Felicity. She tore through the paper and opened it to find a new pair of sturdy boots. "You got me boots!" she squealed in delight.

"Well, I figure you need them now that it's official and all. Those tennis shoes you wear aren't made for winter on the ranch."

She hadn't worn a pair of boots since she'd worked at the lumber mill, and even those had been cheap and uncomfortable. These were a brand that she'd purposely avoided before. The hefty price tag had always warned her to steer clear.

"Thank you. I can't wait to break them in."

Jameson gave Hunter a playful punch on the arm. The two had loosened up around each other in the months since Hunter had proposed.

"Sorry. They told me we were pretty much getting gifts for Felicity since you didn't care for wedding present stuff," Jameson said.

Hunter gave Felicity a grin that melted her bones and said, "I don't mind."

Neither of them cared much for material things, but the gifts their families had given them were so thoughtful.

Camille stood, cradling the side of her belly with a gentle hand. "The last present is from all of us."

"Guys, this is too much," Felicity said.

"Oh, hush," Camille reprimanded. "Let us shower you with gifts on your wedding day."

Felicity chuckled. "Okay, just this once."

Camille handed over a small bag and stepped away.

Inside the bag was a velvet box. Felicity opened it and stared at a pair of familiar diamond earrings.

She gasped and covered her mouth. "Are these Dawn's?"

Camille smiled. "They are. Asa found them at a pawn shop in Cody."

"I can't believe it," Felicity whispered. She rounded on Hunter. "Did you know about this?"

Hunter looked like a cornered cat. "What's the correct answer?"

"The truth."

"I did."

"How long?" she asked.

Hunter scratched his head, tousling his hair. "Since right after I proposed."

That was only two months ago. She had no idea they'd still been looking. She'd written them off as long gone.

She turned back to the room full of people that made up her new family. "Thank you. This is wonderful."

"We know," Haley said. "We love you."

Felicity held the box tight to her chest. "I love you too." Not just her new husband, but all of them.

Levi jumped up. "Let's go see the baby horse!"

ANITA

The last of her boys had been given away. If anyone claimed only wives were given away during a marriage, they'd never married off a son.

Hunter felt as much like hers as any of the others. She'd been happy to open her heart to him from the beginning. She remembered the day he was born. She'd been standing beside his mother when they heard his first cries.

If Butch took everything from them, at least he'd given them Hunter.

He'd never been comfortable as the center of attention, and she'd done well to love him loosely, yet close enough that he never questioned her loyalty.

Today, she wanted to smother him in kisses the way she had when he was a toddler, but she'd keep it to a comforting hug followed by silent tears on the dark drive home.

Silas wrapped an arm around her waist without a word. The king of silence himself knew when her thoughts were spinning.

After hugs and congratulations, they loaded up the gifts and the crowd that made up her family followed each other back to the ranch.

Her cell phone dinged loudly, indicating a message. The bright light from the screen lit up the cab of the truck.

Hunter: Will you meet us at the stables? I want to show Felicity your gift after she names the filly.

Anita rested her hand on Silas's arm. "Hunter wants us to come to the stables."

Silas changed direction. How many times had he driven this path? He was a few months into his sixtieth year, and he belonged to this land as much as the trees. He'd lived his share of back-breaking workdays. Every day, she prayed for another twenty-four hours with the man who had loved her diligently. So far, the Good Lord had seen fit to grant her the requests of her heart.

The ranch was quiet as they entered the stables. The low lighting illuminated her family gathered around a stall toward the middle of the large room. Silas and the men who'd come and gone from this ranch during his time had done a fine job caring for the horses, but her Lucas had put his heart and soul into caring for these animals.

When she'd hired Maddie, Anita had prayed she would be the helpmate her son needed. Thankfully, her motherly instincts had been correct.

Anita watched Maddie rest her cheek against Goldie's mane and said a prayer of thanks for her daughter-in-law.

When Silas and Anita joined the group, Lucas got everyone's attention.

"Okay, it's time for the main event. The naming of the filly." He pointed to Felicity. "Step right up."

"What if she's sleeping? I don't want to bother her," Felicity said as she continued wringing her hands.

"You don't have to go in there. Just get a good look at her and tell us what you think."

Felicity looked back to Hunter who squeezed her shoulder.

Lucas opened the stall door, and everyone stepped closer trying to catch a glimpse of the new horse.

"She's so little," Felicity whispered.

"What do you think?" Hunter asked.

Camille inched closer to Anita's side. When everyone else was interested in the horses, Camille slipped her hand into Anita's.

"We'll have more babies soon," Camille whispered.

Anita's heart swelled, and she squeezed Camille's hand, afraid her voice would shake if she tried to speak.

Maddie wasn't the only wife Anita had predicted for one of her boys. She'd known Camille was the woman for Noah since they were teenagers. They'd had a bond even then that Anita knew was rare and special.

Felicity bunched the sides of her dress into her fists and squatted by the door. "It's so pretty."

"They're not always scary, right?" Maddie said.

"I guess you're right. This one is sweet."

"You have any ideas for a name?" Maddie asked. "You don't have to decide today. I've just been calling her little cutie."

"Actually, I was thinking Hope would be a good name for her."

Haley tucked her chin and cradled her face in her hands as she began to sob. Asher wrapped his arms around her.

Camille sniffled. "It's the hormones."

Haley raised her head and blubbered, "It's so cute, and the name is perfect."

Anita tensed her jaw to keep her chin from quivering. Her kids hadn't seen her cry before, and she wasn't about to start now. She'd quietly cry on Silas's chest tonight before bed, but the tears would be her joy. Her boys had each become part of their new families, but she'd been blessed that each of them had found their place on the ranch.

"Hope," Laney tested the name. "I love it. We aren't short on hope around here."

"I was really hoping she'd name it Sally," Levi added.

Jade tugged the boy to her side with a smile. "You got to name Skittle. I think you're at the bottom of the list to name horses."

"But Skittle is a great name. I think I'm good at naming things."

Anita wondered when Levi would have a little brother or sister. She wouldn't mind a little Sally running around the ranch. Jade had been a perfect addition to their family this year, and she had a mother's heart even before Levi became her own.

Laney patted Micah's chest. "I need to go clean up the kitchen," she whispered to him.

"I'll help." Micah took her hand, and they quietly left the stables.

Micah had stepped into his role as the eldest brother and future leader of the ranch from day one, and Laney was destined to be a wonderful rancher's wife. She had a heart that was open to everyone, and she wasn't afraid of hard work.

Anita rested her head against Silas's shoulder. They'd done well to raise happy children, and they were more than ready for more grandchildren to enjoy.

Gradually, members of her family began to head back to their houses and cabins in groups of two. Aaron carried Levi who rested against his dad's shoulder. Camille and Haley held their bellies and backs as they trudged toward the exit.

Hunter approached Silas and Anita with his hands in his pockets. "Will you come with me to show her?"

"Of course," Anita said. "But it's okay if you want to show her alone."

"No, I'd like for you to be there."

"Then we'll follow you," Silas assured.

Hunter offered a hand to Felicity, and she took it, leaving Lucas and Maddie with the new filly.

"Are you ready for the last gift?" Hunter asked.

Felicity's shoulders slumped. "There's more?"

"Just one more—from Silas and Anita."

Felicity turned to them. "You didn't have to get us anything. You do so much already."

Anita grinned and tilted her head toward the exit. "Let's go."

Silas and Anita followed Hunter's truck out to the place he'd chosen. Noah had helped stake the two-acre parcel earlier today, and as they crested the small rise behind the main house, the solar-powered lights that lined the land Hunter had chosen came into view.

Hunter parked, and Felicity jumped out of the truck. Anita had just opened the truck door when she heard Felicity shout.

"Are you kidding me?"

Hunter met her in front of the truck, and Felicity jumped into his arms. "I can't believe this!"

Silas took Anita's hand, and they slowly walked through the tall grass toward the happy couple. A home is what Felicity needed, and they were happy Hunter would be able to give it to her.

Felicity released Hunter and backed away, surveying the dots of light on the dark hill. "I can't believe this. It's huge!"

"It's two acres," Hunter said. "We can pick a different place, but I thought you'd like this one."

"I can see the main house. No, this spot is perfect," Felicity confirmed.

A tear slid down Anita's cheek, and she was thankful for the darkness. She'd been worried that Hunter and Felicity would isolate themselves, but it seemed Felicity was clinging to her new family—the one she never had before now.

When Felicity had turned in circles and studied the spot where she and Hunter would build their new home, she caught sight of Anita and Silas.

Felicity walked straight to Anita. "Thank you."

Anita couldn't speak. She was grateful Felicity loved her Hunter the way he deserved. Anita was the thankful one.

Felicity wrapped her arms around Anita and whispered in her ear, "I love you, Mama."

"I love you too." Anita meant every word.

Felicity's mom hadn't been good to her, but Anita would be there for her until the end.

Hunter took his place at Felicity's side as she released Anita from their hug. He wrapped his arms around his new bride and kissed the side of her head.

Hunter and Felicity had forever to share love between them, and today was only the beginning.

HUNTER

Hunter opened the passenger door of the truck, and Felicity tucked the flowing skirt of her dress around her legs as she slid into the seat. She was gorgeous on a regular day, but she'd been stealing his breath all evening.

It wasn't her dress. It was her smile and those two words that bound them together for the rest of their lives.

He closed the door and walked around the front of the truck. Silas and Anita were just driving away, back to the main house. They'd put the icing on the cake tonight, and he was glad Felicity knew who would always be in their corner.

The lights in the cab came on as he took his place behind the wheel. Felicity leaned over the console wearing that knock-out smile that hit him square in the chest every time.

"What are you smiling about?" she asked.

Hunter started the truck. "Am I?" He hadn't noticed, but it sounded about right. He'd never worried about heart palpitations until Felicity came around and the strange physical reactions began. She could walk into a room, and he'd forget what he was doing. She'd look his way, and his fingers would tingle and beg to reach for her hair.

Crazy things.

"You look like you just stole a cookie," she said.

Hunter linked his fingers through hers and lifted her hand to kiss the soft skin on the back. "I think I'm just a happily married man."

"Can you even believe what you're saying? We're *married.*"

No, he couldn't believe it. He'd just stepped out of his quiet and lonely world into a life of marital bliss with the perfect woman. If he hadn't been standing there when Jameson gave her away, he'd swear it was all a dream.

He parked the truck in front of her cabin and shut it off. Without the diesel engine noise, the summer night was peaceful.

Felicity looked over her shoulder at the path they'd just driven. "Is it weird that I want to go back?" she whispered.

Hunter leaned in and kissed her rounded cheek, then the exposed skin of her neck, then the soft terrain of her collarbone. "Can I at least carry you over the threshold first?"

Felicity's eyes widened. "Hunter Harding, I had no idea you were such a romantic."

"I only get one wedding night. I'm pulling out all the stops."

"Oh! You didn't take off my garter! That's a thing at weddings."

Hunter opened the truck door and jumped out. He jogged around the truck to her side and swept her into his arms. "I can fix that."

Felicity laughed. "You were supposed to do it at the reception."

Hunter fought the urge to jog onto the porch and through the door. In the dark, he was bound to trip and send both of them flying. "And then throw it to the single men. I know. All my cousins had weddings. But there weren't any single men at our reception."

"Jameson."

"Okay, can we just pretend that Jameson is getting married next according to the garter throwing tradition?"

Felicity squeezed her arms tighter around his neck as he fumbled for the doorknob. "I don't care about all the things that go on during weddings. I'm sure they're fun, but I'm just glad we were married in a church before God and our families. That's all I ever wanted."

Hunter nudged the old wooden door open and stepped over the threshold with his wife in his arms. "You're all I ever wanted."

THE END

About the Author

Mandi Blake was born and raised in Alabama where she lives with her husband and daughter, but her southern heart loves to travel. Reading has been her favorite hobby for as long as she can remember, but writing is her passion. She loves a good happily ever after in her sweet Christian romance books and loves to see her characters' relationships grow closer to God and each other.

Made in the USA
Columbia, SC
07 August 2021

43169127R00176